THE VOICE
ON THE WIRE

Eustace Hale Ball

1st WORLD
LIBRARY
Literary Society

The Voice on the Wire

Eustace Hale Ball

© 1st World Library – Literary Society, 2005
PO Box 2211
Fairfield, IA 52556
www.1stworldlibrary.org
First Edition

LCCN: 2006902693

Softcover ISBN: 1-4218-1826-4
Hardcover ISBN: 1-4218-1726-8
eBook ISBN: 1-4218-1926-0

Purchase *"The Voice on the Wire"*
as a traditional bound book at:
www.1stWorldLibrary.org/purchase.asp?ISBN=1-4218-1826-4

1st World Library Literary Society is a nonprofit
organization dedicated to promoting literacy by:

- Creating a free internet library accessible from any
  computer worldwide.
- Hosting writing competitions and offering book
  publishing scholarships.

The Voice on the Wire
contributed by Tim, Ed & Rodney
in support of
1st World Library Literary Society

CHAPTER I

WHEN THREE IS A MYSTERY

"Mr. Shirley is waiting for you in the grill-room, sir. Just step this way, sir, and down the stairs."

The large man awkwardly followed the servant to the cosey grill-room on the lower floor of the club house. He felt that every man of the little groups about the Flemish tables must be saying: "What's he doing here?"

"I wish Monty Shirley would meet me once in a while in the back room of a ginmill, where I'd feel comfortable," muttered the unhappy visitor. "This joint is too classy. But that's his game to play -"

He reached the sought-for one, however, and exclaimed eagerly: "By Jiminy, Monty. I'm glad to find you - it would have been my luck after this day, to get here too late."

He was greeted with a grip that made even his generous hand wince, as the other arose to smile a welcome.

"Hello, Captain Cronin. You're a good sight for a grouchy man's eyes! Sit down and confide the brand of your particular favorite poison to our Japanese Dionysius!"

The Captain sighed with relief, as he obeyed.

"Bar whiskey is good enough for an old timer like me. Don't tell me you have the blues - your face isn't built that way!"

"Gospel truth, Captain. I've been loafing around this club - nothing to do for a month. Bridge, handball, highballs, and yarns! I'm actually a nervous wreck because my nerves haven't had any work to do!"

"You're the healthiest invalid I've seen since the hospital days in the Civil War. But don't worry about something to do. I've some job now. It's dolled up with all them frills you like: millions, murders and mysteries! If this don't keep you awake, you'll have nightmares for the next six months. Do you want it?"

"I'm tickled to death. Spill it!"

"Monty, it's the greatest case my detective agency has had since I left the police force eleven years ago. It's too big for me, and I've come to you to do a stunt as is a stunt. You will plug it for me, won't you - just as you've always done? If I get the credit, it'll mean a fortune to me in the advertising alone."

"Haven't I handled every case for you in confidence. I'm not a fly-cop, Captain Cronin. I'm a consulting specialist, and there's no shingle hung out. Perhaps you had better take it to some one else."

Shirley pushed away his empty glass impatiently.

"There, Monty, I didn't mean to offend you. But there's such swells in this and such a foxey bunch of blacklegs, that I'm as nervous as a rookie cop on his first arrest. Don't hold a grudge against me."

Shirley lit a cigarette and resumed his good nature: "Go on, Captain. I'm so stale with dolce far niente, after the Black Pearl affair last month, that I act like an amateur myself. Make it short, though, for I'm going to the opera."

The Captain leaned over the table, his face tense with suppressed emotion. He was a grizzled veteran of the New York police force: a man who sought his quarry with the ferocity of a bull-dog, when the line of search was definitely assured. Lacking imagination and the subtler senses of criminology, Captain Cronin had built up a reputation for success and honesty in every assignment by bravery, persistence, and as in this case, the ability to cover his own deductive weakness by employing the brains of others.

Montague Shirley was as antithetical from the veteran detective as a man could well be. A noted athlete in his university, he possessed a society rating in New York, at Newport and Tuxedo, and on the Continent which was the envy of many a gilded youth born to the purple.

On leaving college, despite an ample patrimony, he had curiously enough entered the lists as a newspaper man. From the sporting page he was graduated to police news, then the city desk, at last closing his career as the genius who invented the weekly Sunday thriller, in many colors of illustration and vivacious Gallic style which interpreted into heart throbs and goose-flesh the real life romances and tragedies of the preceding six days! He had conquered the paper-and-ink world - then deep within there stirred the call for participation in the game itself.

So, dropping quietly into the apparently indolent routine of club existence, he had devoted his experience and genius to analytical criminology - a line of endeavor known only to five men in the world.

He maintained no offices. He wore no glittering badges: a police card, a fire badge, and a revolver license, renewed year after year, were the only instruments of his trade ever in evidence. Shirley took assignments only from the heads of certain agencies, by personal arrangement as informal as this from Captain Cronin. His real clients never knew of his participation, and his prey never understood that he had been the real head-hunter!

His fees - Montague Shirley, as a master craftsman deemed his artistry worthy of the hire. His every case meant a modest fortune to the detective agency and Shirley's bills were never rendered, but always paid!

So, here, the hero of the gridiron and the class re-union, the gallant of a hundred pre-matrimonial and non-maturing engagements, the veteran of a thousand drolleries and merry jousts in clubdom - unspoiled by birth, breeding and wealth, untrammeled by the juggernaut of pot-boiling and the salary-grind, had drifted into the curious profession of confidential, consulting criminal chaser.

Shirley unostentatiously signaled for an encore on the refreshments.

"You're nervous to-night, Captain. You've been doing things before you consulted me - which is against our Rule Number One, isn't it?"

The Captain gulped down his whiskey, and rubbed his forehead.

"Couldn't help it, Monty. It got too busy for me, before I realized anything unusual in the case. See what I got from a gangster before I landed here."

He turned his close-cropped head, as Montague Shirley leaned forward to observe an abrasion at the base of his skull. It was dressed with a coating of collodion.

"Brass knuckled - I see the mark of the rings. Tried for the pneumogastric nerves, to quiet you."

"Whatever he tried for he nearly got. Kelly's nightstick got his pneumonia gas jet, or whatever you call it. He's still quiet, in the station house - You know old man Van Cleft, who owns sky-scrapers down town, don't you? - Well, he's the center of this flying wedge of excitement. His family are fine people, I understand. His daughter was to be married next week. Monty, that wedding'll be postponed, and old Van Cleft won't worry over dispossess papers for his tenants for the rest of the winter. See?"

"Killed?"

"Correct. He's done, and I had a hell of a time getting the body home, before the coroner and the police reporters got on the trail."

Shirley lowered his high-ball glass, with an earnest stare.

"What was the idea?"

"Robbery, of course. His son had me on the case - 'phoned from the garage where the chauffeur brought the body; after he saw the old man unconscious. Just half an hour before he had left his office in the same machine, after taking five thousand dollars in cash from his manager."

"Who was with him?"

"Now, that's getting to brass tacks. When I gets that C.Q.D. from Van Cleft, I finds the young fellow inside the ring of rubbernecks, blubbering over the old man, where he lies on the floor of the taxi - looking soused."

"He was a notorious old sport about town, Captain."

"Sure - and I thinks, it sorter serves him right. But, that's his funeral, not mine. Van Cleft, junior, says to me: 'There's the girl that was with him.'"

"Where was the girl?"

"She was sitting on a stool, near the car, a little blonde chorus chicken, shaking and twitching, while the chauffeur and the garage boss held her up. I says, 'What's this?' and Van Cleft tells me all he knows, which ain't nothing. Them guys in that garage was wise, for it meant a cold five hundred apiece before I left to keep their lids closed. Van Cleft begs me to hustle the old man home, so one of my men takes her down to my office, still a sniffling, and acting like she had the D.T.'s. The young fellow shook like a leaf, but we takes him over to Central Park East, to the family mansion, - carrying him up the steps like he was drunk. We gets him into his own bed, and keeps the sister from touching his clammy hands, while she orders the family doctor. When he gets there on the jump, I gives him the wink and leads him to one side. 'Doc,' I says, 'you know how to write out a death certificate, to hush this up from your end. I've done the rest.'"

Captain Cronin leaned forward, a queer excitement agitating him.

"Do you know what that doctor says to me, Monty?"

Shirley shook his head.

He says; "My God, it's the third!"

Shirley's white hand gripped the edge of the table. "The Van Cleft's doctor is one of the greatest surgeons in the country, Professor MacDonald of the Medical College. He said that?"

"He did. I answers, 'Whadd'y mean the third?' Then he looks me straight in the eye, and sings back, 'None of your business.'" Cronin shook his head. "I never seen a man with a squarer look, and yet he has me guessing. I goes back to the garage, over past Eighth Avenue, you know, where two johns come up along side o' me. One rubs me with his elbow and the other applies that brass knuckle, - then they gets pinched. I got dressed up in a drug store, got the chauffeur's license number, and goes on down to my office to see this girl. She's hysterical about his family using all their money to put her in jail. I looks at her, and says, 'You won't need their money to get to jail. That old man's dead!' Her eyes was as big as saucers. 'I thought old Daddy Van Cleft was drunk.' I tells her, 'He was dead in that taxi, with a chorus girl, and a roll of bills gone. What you got to say?' She staggers forward and clutches my coat, and what do you think SHE says to me?"

Shirley made the inquiry only with his eyes, puffing his cigarette slowly.

"She looks sorter green, and repeats after me: 'Dead, with a chorus girl, and a roll of bills gone,' - just like a parrot. Then she springs this on me: 'My God, it's the third!'"

Shirley dropped his cigarette, leaning forward, all nonchalance gone.

"Where is she now? Quick, let's go to her."

He rose to his feet. Just then a door-boy walked through the grill-room toward him. "A telephone call for Captain Cronin, sir; the party said hurry or he would miss something good."

Shirley snapped out, "When has the rule about telephone calls in this club been changed? You boys are never to tell any one that a member or guest are here until the name is announced."

He turned toward the puzzled Captain.

"Did you ask any of your operatives to call you here? You know what a risk you are taking, to connect me with this case like that, don't you?"

"I never even breathed it to myself. I told no one."

"Follow me up to the telephone room."

Shirley hurried through the grill, to the switchboard, near which stood the booths for private calls. He called to one of the operators. "Here, let me at that switchboard." He pushed the boy aside, and sat down in the vacated chair.

"Which trunk is it on? Oh, I see, the second. There Captain, take the fourth booth against the wall."

Cronin stepped in. Shirley connected up and listened with the transmitter of the operator at his ear, holding the line open.

"Go ahead, here's Captain Cronin!"

A pleasant voice came over the wire. It was musical and sincere.

"Hello, Captain Cronin, is that you?"

"Yes! What do you want?"

The voice continued, with a jolly laugh, ringing and infectious in its merriment.

"Well, Captain, the joke's on you. Ha, ha, ha! It's a bully one! Ho, ho! Ha, ha!"

"What joke?"

"You're working on the Van Cleft case. Oh, sure, you are, don't kid me back. Well, Captain, you've missed two other perfectly good grafts. This is the third one!"

There was a click and the speaker, with another merry gurgle, rang off.

"Quick, manager's desk," cried Shirley, jiggling the metal key. "What call was that? Where did it come from?"

After a little wait, a languid voice answered: "Brooklyn, Main 6969, Party C."

"Give me the number again - I want to speak on the wire."

After another delay, the voice replied "The line has been discontinued."

"I just had it! What is the name of the subscriber. Hurry, this is a matter of life and death."

"It's against the rules to give any further information. But our record shows that the house burned down about two weeks ago. No one else has been given the number. There's no instrument there!"

CHAPTER II

THE FLEETING PROMPTER

Monty's puzzled smile was in no wise reciprocated by the Captain, whose red face evidenced a growing resentment.

He began a tirade, but a wink from the club man warned him. Shirley replaced the receiver, and the regular attendant resumed his place at the switchboard. The lad was curious at the unusual ability of the wealthy Mr. Shirley to handle the bewildering maze of telephone attachments. Monty explained, as he turned to go upstairs.

"Son, that was one of my smart friends trying to play a practical joke on my guest. I fooled him. Don't let it happen again, until you send in the party's name first."

"Yes, sir," meekly promised the boy.

"Well, Captain Cronin, as the old paperback novels used to say at the end of the first instalment, 'The Plot thickens!' At first I thought this case of stupid badger game - "

"You aren't going to back out, Monty? Here's a whole gang of crooks which would give you some sport rounding up, and as for money - "

"Money is easy, from both sides of a criminal matter. What interests me is that ghostly telephone call from a house that

Eustace Hale Ball

burned down, and the caller's knowledge of Number Three. I'm in this case, have no fear of that."

Shirley led his guest to the coat room.

"I'll get a taxicab, Monty. We'd better see that girl first and then have a look at the body."

The Captain turned to the door, as the attendant helped Monty with his overcoat. The waiter from the grill-room approached. "Excuse me, sir, but the gentleman dropped his handkerchief in his chair opposite you."

"Thank you, Gordon," he said, as he faced the servant for an instant. When he turned again, toward the front hall, the Captain had passed out of view through the front door.

Shirley received a surprise when he reached the pavement on Forty-fourth Street, for Captain Cronin was not in sight. Two club men descended the steps of the neighboring house. Others strolled along toward the Avenue, but not a sign of a vehicle of any description could be seen, nor was there anything suspicious in view. Cronin had disappeared as effectually as though he had taken a passing Zeppelin!

"I'm glad this affair will not bore me," murmured the criminologist, as he evolved and promptly discarded a dozen vain theories to explain the disappearance of his companion.

Twenty minutes were wasted along the block, as he waited for some sight or sign. Then he decided to go on up to Van Cleft's residence. But, realizing the probability of "shadow" work upon all who came from the door of the club, after the curious message on the wire, Shirley did not propose to expose his hand. Walking leisurely to the Avenue, he hailed a passing hansom. He directed the driver to carry him to an address on Central Park West. His shrewdness was not wasted, for as he stepped into the vehicle, he espied a slinking figure crossing the street diagonally before him, to disappear into the shadow of an adjacent doorway. This was the house of Reginald Van Der Voor, as Shirley knew. It was closed because its master, a social acquaintance of the club man's, was at this time touring the Orient in his steam yacht. No man should have entered that doorway. So, as the horse started under the flick of the long whip, Shirley peered unobserved through the glass window at his side.

A big machine swung up behind the hansom, at some unseen hail, and the figure came from the doorway, leaping into the car, as it followed Shirley up the Avenue, a block or so behind.

"It is not always so easy to follow, when the leader knows his chase," thought Shirley. "I'm glad I'm only a simple club man."

The automobile was unmistakably trailing him, as the hansom crossed the Plaza, then sped through the Park drive, to the address he had given his driver.

As Shirley had remembered, this was a large apartment house, in which one of his bachelor friends lived. He knew the lay of the building well: next door, with an entrance facing on the side street was another just like it, and of equal height.

"Wait for me, here," said Shirley. "I'll pay you now, but want to go to an address down town in five minutes."

He gave the driver a bill, then entered and told the elevator man to take him to the ninth floor.

"There's nobody in, boss," began the boy. But Shirley shook his head.

"My friend is expecting me for a little card game, that's why you think he is out. Just take me up."

He handed the negro a quarter, which was complete in its logic.

As he reached the floor, he waved to the elevator operator. "Go on down, and don't let any one else come up, for Mr. Greenough doesn't want company."

As the car slid down, Shirley fumbled along the familiar hall to the iron stairs which led to the roof of the building. Up these he hurried, thence out upon the roof. It was a matter of only four minutes before he had crossed to the next apartment building, opened the door of the roof-entry, found the stairs to the ninth floor, and taken this elevator to the street.

He walked out of the building, and turned toward Central Park West, to slyly observe the entrance of the building where waited the faithful hansom Jehu. A young man was in conversation with the driver, and the big automobile could be seen on the other side of the street awaiting further developments.

"He has a long vigil there," laughed Shirley. "Now, for the real address. I think I lost the hounds for this time."

Another vehicle took him through the Park to the darkened mansion of the Van Clefts'. Here, Shirley's card brought a quick response from the surprised son of the dead millionaire.

"Why - why - I'm glad to see you, Mr. Shirley - Who sent you?" he began.

Shirley registered complete surprise. "Sent me, my dear Van Cleft? Who should send me? For what? It just happened that I was walking up the Avenue, and to-morrow night I plan to give a little farewell supper to Hal Bingley, class of '03, at the club You knew him in College? I thought you might like to come."

"Step in the library," requested Van Cleft, weakly. "Sit down, Mr. Shirley - I'm upset to-night."

He mopped his brow with a damp handkerchief, and Shirley's

big heart went out to the young chap, as he saw the haggard lines of horror and grief on his usually pleasant face.

"What's the trouble, old man? Anything I can do?"

"My father just died this evening, and I'm in awful trouble - I thought it was the Coroner, or the police - " he bit his tongue as the last words escaped him. Shirley put his hand on Van Cleft's shoulder, with an inspiring firmness.

"Tell me how I can help. You've had a big shock. Confide in me, and I pledge you my word, I'll keep it safer than any one you could go to."

Van Cleft groped as a drowning man, at this opportunity. He caught Shirley's hand and wrung it tensely.

"Sit down. The doctor is still upstairs with mother and sister. When the Coroner comes, I would like to have you be here as a witness. It's an ordeal - I'll tell you everything."

Shirley listened attentively, without betraying his own knowledge. Soothing in manner, he questioned the son about any possible enemy of the murdered man.

"There's not one I know. Dad is popular - he's been too gay, lately, but just foolish like a lot of rich men. He wouldn't harm any one. He inherited his money, you know. Didn't have to crush the working people. Like me, he's been endeavoring to spend it ever since he was born, but it comes in too fast from our estates."

He looked up apprehensively, at the sympathetic face of his companion.

"It's very unwise to tell this. I suppose it's a State's prison offence to deceive about murder. But you understand our position: we can't afford to let it become gossip. I'll pay this girl anything to go to Europe or the Antipodes!"

"I wouldn't do that," suggested Shirley, thoughtfully. "Let her stay. You would like to bring the culprit to justice, if it can be done without dragging your name into it. If he has planned this, he has executed other schemes. She certainly would not remain the machine if she were the guilty one. Why not employ a good detective?"

"I did, but hesitated to tell you. I secured Captain Cronin, of the Holland Agency. He's managed everything so far - I was too rattled myself. But, I wonder why he isn't here now? He was to return as soon as he visited the garage."

As Van Cleft spoke, the butler approached with hesitation.

"Beg pardon, sir. But you are wanted on the telephone, sir."

"All right, Hoskins. Connect it with the library instrument."

Van Cleft lifted the receiver nervously, and answered in an unsteady voice.

"Yes - This is Van Cleft's residence."

Silence for a bit, then the wire was busy.

"What's that? Captain Cronin? What about him? Let me speak to him."

Shirley was alert as a cat. Van Cleft was too dazed to understand his sudden move, as the criminologist caught up the receiver, and placed his palm for an instant over the mouthpiece.

"Ask him to say it again - that you didn't understand." Shirley removed his hand, and obeyed. Shirley held the receiver to his ear, as the young man spoke. Then he heard these curious words: "You poor simp, you'd better get that family doctor of yours to give you some ear medicine, and stop wasting time with the death certificate. I told you that Cronin was over in

Bellevue Hospital with a fractured skull. Unless you drop this investigating, you'll get one, too. Ta, ta! Old top!"

The receiver was hung up quickly at the other end of the line.

Shirley gave a quick call for "Information," and after several minutes learned that the call came from a drug store pay-station in Jersey City!

The melodious tones were unmistakably those of the speaker who had used the wire from faraway Brooklyn where the house had been burned down! It was a human impossibility for any one to have covered the distance between the two points in this brief time, except in an aeroplane!

Van Cleft wondered dumbly at his companion's excitement. Shirley caught up the telephone again.

"Some one says that Cronin is at Bellevue Hospital, injured. I'll find out."

It was true. Captain Cronin was lying at point of death, the ward nurse said, in answer to his eager query. At first the ambulance surgeon had supposed him to be drunk, for a patrolman had pulled him out of a dark doorway, unconscious.

"Where was the doorway? This is his son speaking, so tell me all."

"Just a minute. Oh! Here is the report slip. He was taken from the corner of Avenue A and East Eleventh Street. You'd better come down right away, for he is apt to die tonight. He's only been here ten minutes."

"Has any one else telephoned to find out about him?"

"No. We didn't even know his name until just as you called up, when we found his papers and some warrants in a pocketbook. How did you know?"

But Shirley disconnected curtly, this time. He bowed his head in thought, and then, with his usual nervous custom, fumbled for a cigarette. Here was the Captain, whom he had left on Forty-fourth Street, near Fifth Avenue, a short time before, discovered fully three miles away.

And the news telephoned from Jersey City, by the fleeting magic voice on the wire. Even his iron composure was stirred by this weird complication.

"I wonder!" he murmured. He had ample reason to wonder.

CHAPTER III

THE INNOCENT BYSTANDER

"Well, Mr. Shirley, your coming here was a Godsend! I don't know what to do now. The newspapers will get this surely. I depended on Cronin: he must have been drinking."

Shirley shook his head, as he explained, "I know Cronin's reputation, for I was a police reporter. He is a sterling man. There's foul work here which extends beyond your father's case. But we are wasting time. Why don't you introduce me to your physician? Just tell him about Cronin, and that you have confided in me completely."

Van Cleft went upstairs without a word. Unused to any worry, always able to pay others for the execution of necessary details, this young man was a victim of the system which had engulfed his unfortunate sire in the maelstrom of reckless pleasure.

By his ingenuous adroitness, it may be seen, Shirley was inveigling himself into the heart of the affair, in his favorite disguise as that of the "innocent bystander." His innate dramatic ability assisted him in maintaining his friendly and almost impersonal role, with a success which had in the past kept the secret of his system from even the evildoers themselves.

"A little investigation of the telephone exchanges during the next day or two will not be wasted time," he mused. "I'll get

Eustace Hale Ball

Sam Grindle, their assistant advertising manager to show me the way the wheels go 'round. No man can ride a Magic Carpet of Bagdad over the skyscrapers in these days of shattered folklore."

Howard Van Cleft returned with the famous surgeon, Professor MacDonald. He was elderly, with the broad high forehead, dignity of poise, and sharpness of glance which bespeaks the successful scientist. His face, to-night, was chalky and the firm, full mouth twitched with nervousness. He greeted Shirley abstractedly. The criminologist's manner was that of friendly anxiety.

"You are here, sir, as a friend of the family?"

"Yes. Howard has told me of the terrible mystery of this case. As an ex-newspaper man I imagine that my influence and friendships may keep the unpleasant details from the press."

"That is good," sighed the doctor, with relief. "How soon will you do it?"

"Now, using this telephone. No, for certain reasons, I had better use an outside instrument. I will call up men I know on each paper, as though this were a 'scoop,' so that knowing me, they will be confident that I tell them the truth as a favor. Such deceit is excusable under the circumstances. It may eventually bring the murderer to justice."

Professor MacDonald winced at the word. He turned toward Van Cleft, on sudden thought, remarking: "Howard your mother and sister may need the comfort of your presence. I will chat with your friend until the Coroner comes."

The physician sank into a library chair. The criminologist quietly awaited his cue. He lit a cigarette and the minutes drifted past with no word between them. The doctor's gaze lowered to the vellum-bound books on the carven table, then to the gorgeous pattern of the Kermansha at his feet. Once more he studied the face of his companion, with the keen, soul-gripping scrutiny of the skilled physician. As last he arrived at a definite conclusion. He cleared his throat, and fumbled in his waistcoat pocket for a cigar. A swiftly struck match in Monty's hand was held up so promptly to the end of the cigar, that the doctor's lips had not closed about it. This deftness, simple in itself, did not escape the observation of the scientist. He smiled for the first time during their interview.

"Your reflex nerves are very wide awake for a quiet man. I believe I can depend upon those nerves, and your quietude. May I ask what occupation you follow, if any? Most of Howard's friends follow butterflies."

"I am one of them, then. Some opera, more theatricals, much art gallery touring. A little regular reading in my rooms, and there you are! My great grandfather was too poor a trader to succeed in pelts, so he invested a little money in rocky pastures around upper Manhattan: this has kept the clerks of the family bankers busy ever since. I am an optimistic vagabond, enjoying life in the observation of the rather ludicrous busyness of other folk. In short, Doctor, I am a corpulent Hamlet, essentially modern in my cultivation of a joy in life, debating the eternal question with myself, but lazily leaving it to others to solve. Therein I am true to my type."

"Pardon my bluntness," observed MacDonald, watching him through partially closed eyes. "You are not telling the truth. You are a busy man, with definite work, but that is no affair of mine. I recognize in you a different calibre from that of these rich young idlers in Howard's class. I am going to take you into my confidence, for you understand the need for secrecy, and will surely help in every way - noblesse oblige. This man Cronin, the detective, was rather crude."

"He is honest and dependable," replied Shirley, loyally.

"Yes, but I wonder why professional detectives are so primitive. They wear their calling cards and their business shingles on their figures and faces. Surely the crooks must know them all personally. I read detective stories, in rest moments, and every one of the sleuths lives in some well-known apartment, or on a prominent street. Some day we may read of one who is truly in secret service, but not until after his death notice. But there, I am talking to quiet my own nerves a bit, - now we will get to cases."

The doctor dropped his cigar into the bronze tray on the table, leaning forward with intense earnestness, as he continued.

"This, Mr. Shirley, is the third murder of the sort within a week. Wellington Serral, the wealthy broker, came to a sudden death in a private dining room last Monday, in the company of a young show girl. He was a patient of mine, and I signed the death certificate as heart failure, to save the honorable family name for his two orphaned daughters.

"Herbert de Cleyster, the railroad magnate, died similarly in a taxicab on Thursday. He was also one of my patients. There, too, was concerned another of these wretched chorus girls. To-night the fatal number of the triad was consummated in this cycle of crime. To maintain my loyalty to my patients I have risked my professional reputation. Have I done wrong?"

"No! The criminal shall be brought to justice," replied Shirley in a voice vibrant with a profound determination which was not lost upon his companion.

"Are you powerful enough to bring this about, without disgracing me or betraying this sordid tragedy to the morbid scandal-rakers of the papers?"

"I will devote every waking hour to it. But, like you, my efforts must remain entirely secret. I vow to find this man before I sleep again!"

"You are determined - yet it cannot be one single man. It must be an organized gang, for all the crimes have been so strangely similar, occurring to three men who are friends, and entrez nous, notorious for their peccadilloes. The girls must be in the vicious circle, and ably assisted. But there is one thing I forgot to tell you, which you forgot to ask."

"And this is?"

"How they died. It was by some curious method of sudden arterial stoppage. Old as they were, some fiendish trick was employed so skilfully that the result was actual heart failure. There was no trace of drugs in lungs or blood. On each man's breast, beneath the sternum bone I found a dull, barely discernible bruise mark, which I later removed by a simple massage of the spot!"

Shirley closed his eyes, and passed his hand over his own chest - along the armpits - behind his ears - he seemed to be mentally enumerating some list of nerve centers. The physician observed him curiously.

"I have it, doctor! The sen-si-yao!"

"What do you mean?"

"The most powerful and secret of all the death-strokes of the Japanese art of jiu-jitsu fighting. I paid two thousand dollars to learn the course from a visiting instructor when I was in college. It was worth it for this one occasion."

Shirley arose to his feet, and approached the other, touching his shoulder.

"Stand up, if you please. Let me ask if this was the location of the mark?"

The physician, interested in this new professional phase, readily obeyed. One quick movement of Shirley's muscular hand, the thumb oddly twisted and stiffened, and a sudden jab in the doctor's abdomen made that gentleman gasp with pain.

Eustace Hale Ball

Shirley's expression was triumphant, but the professor regarded him with an expression of terror.

"Oh! Ugh! - What-did-you-do-to me?" he murmured thickly, when he was at last able to speak.

"Merely demonstrated the beginning of the death punch which I named. That pressure if continued for half a minute would have been fatal."

"I wish you would teach me that," was the physician's natural request, as he nodded with a wry face.

"Impossible, my dear sir, for I learned it, according to the Oriental custom under the most sacred obligations of secrecy. One must advance through the whole course, by initiatory degrees, before learning the final mysteries of the samurais. Now, we have a working hypothesis. The girls could never have accomplished this. One man and one alone must have killed the three, although doubtless with confederates. Yamashino assured me that there were only six men in this country who knew it beside myself. We must find an Orientalist!"

Shirley paced the floor, but his meditations were interrupted by the arrival of the Coroner and his physician. Van Cleft hurried into the room with them, to present the doctor, who exchanged a formal greeting with the men he had met twice before that week.

"A sad affair, Professor," observed the Coroner nervously, drinking in with profound respect the magnificent surroundings which symbolized the great wealth of which he secretly hoped to gain a tithing. "I trust that, as usual, in such cases, I may suggest an undertaker?"

"Why - talk about that at once, sir?" asked Howard with a shudder.

The physician, familiar with the subtleties of coroners, gently placed an arm about the young man's shoulder. He nodded, understandingly, to the Coroner, as he turned toward Shirley.

"I must be going now," the latter interposed. "Just a word with you, Howard, that I may send a message to your mother and sister."

The physician led away the two officials as Shirley continued: "I must go to see Cronin - deserted there like a run-over mongrel on the street. Can I leave this house by the rear, so that none shall know of my assistance in the case, or follow me to the hospital? If you can secure an old hat and coat, I will leave my own, with my stick, to get them some other time."

"I will get some from the butler, if you wait just a moment. You can leave by the rear yard, if you don't mind climbing a high board fence."

Van Cleft hurried downstairs, in a few minutes, bearing a weather-beaten overcoat and an English cap, which Shirley drew down over his ears. With the coat on, he looked very unlike the well-groomed club man who had entered. Unseen by Van Cleft he shifted an automatic revolver into the coat pocket from the discarded garment.

"Now, Mr. Shirley, come this way. Follow the rear area-way, across to the next yard, where after another climb you find a vacant lot where the Schuylers are preparing to erect their new city house. Will you attend to everything?"

"Everything. I'll start sooner than you expect."

Truly he did! For no sooner had he descended the second fence into the empty lot than a stinging blow sent him at full length on the rocky ground, where the excavations were already being started. Two men pounced upon him in a twinkling - only his great strength, acquired through the football years, saved him from immediate defeat. His head throbbed, and he was dizzy as he caught the wrist of the nearest assailant with a quick twist which resulted in a sudden, sickening crunch. The man groaned in agony, but his companion kicked with heavy-shod feet at the prostrate man. Shirley's left hand duplicated the vice-like grip upon the ankle of the standing assailant, and his deftness caused another tendon strain! Both men toppled to the ground, now, and before they realized it Shirley had reversed the advantage. His automatic emphasized his superiority of tactics. He understood their silence, broken only by muted groans: they feared the police, even as did he, although for different reasons. He "frisked" the man nearest him upon the ground, and captured deftly the rascal's weapon: then he sprang up covering the twain.

"Get up! Youse guys is poachin' in de wrong district - dis belongs to de Muggins gang. I'll fix youse guys fer buttin' in. Up, dere!" His hands went into his coat pockets, but the men knew that they were still pointing at them, the gunman's "cover" as it is called. They staggered sullenly to their feet. He beckoned with his head, toward the front of the lot. They followed the silent instructions, one limping while his mate wrung the injured wrist in agony.

Directly before the lot stood a throbbing, empty automobile. Shirley decided to take another car - he could not guard them and drive at the same time.

"Down to Fift' Avnoo," he ordered. "I got two guns - not a woid from youse!" His erstwhile amiable physiognomy, now gnarled into an unrecognizable mask of low villainy bespoke his desperate earnestness. The men obeyed. This was apparently a gangster, of gangsters - their fear of the dire vengeance of a rival organization of cut-throats instilled an obedience more humble than any other threats.

Toward the Park side they advance, one leaning heavily upon the other. Shirley, his broad shoulders hunched up; with the collar drawn high about his neck, the murderous looking cap down over his eyes, followed them doggedly.

A big limousine was speeding down the Avenue from some homing theater party. Shirley hailed it with an authoritive yell which caused the chauffeur to put on a quick brake.

"Git out dere, - no gun play. Up inter dat car!" he added, as they approached the machine.

"Say, what you drivin' at?" cried the driver, queruously. "Is this a hold-up?" It was a puzzling moment, but the criminologist's calm bravado saved the situation: as luck would have it no policemen were in sight, to spoil the maneuver.

"No," and he assumed a more natural voice and dialect. "I'm a detective. These men were just house-breaking, and I got them. There's twenty-five dollars in it for you, if you take us down to the Holland Detective Agency, in ten minutes."

"He's kiddin' ye, feller," snapped out one man.

"Don't fall fen him, yen boob!" sung out the other.

But Shirley's automatic now appeared outside the coat pocket. The chauffeur realized that here was serious gaming. With his left hand Shirley jerked out the ever ready police card and fire badge, which seemed official enough to satisfy the driver.

"Quick now, or I'll run you in, too, for refusing to obey an officer. You men climb into that back seat. Driver, beat it now to Thirty-nine West Forty Street, if you need that twenty-five dollars. I'll sit with them. I don't want any interference so I can come back and nab the rest of their gang."

His authoritative manner convinced this new ally, and he climbed into the car, facing his prisoners, with the two weapons held down below the level of the windows. Pedestrians and other motorists little recked what strange cargo was borne as the car raced down the broad thoroughfare.

Eustace Hale Ball

In nine minutes they drew up before the Holland Agency, a darkened, brown front house of ancient architecture. The chauffeur sprang out to swing back the door.

"Go up the steps, and tell the doorman that Captain Cronin wants two men to bring down their guns and handcuffs and get two prisoners. Quick!"

The street was not empty, even at this hour. Yet the passersby did not realize the grim drama enacted inside the waiting machine. Hours seemed to pass before Cronin's men returned with the driver, as much surprised by the three strange faces within the machine, as he had been.

"You take these men upstairs and keep them locked up," bluntly commanded the criminologist. "They're nabbed on the new case of the Captain's which started to-night, I'm going over to Bellevue to see him." His voice was still disguised, his features twisted even yet.

The men gave him a curious glance, and then obeyed. As they disappeared behind the heavy wooden door, Shirley stepped into a dark hallway, close by. He lit a wax match to give him light for the choosing of the right amount, from the roll of bills which he drew forth. The chauffeur whistled with surprise at the size of the denominations. The twenty-five were handed over.

"Thanks very much, my friend," and the face unsnarled itself, into the amiable lines of the normal. The voice was agreeable and smooth, which surprised the man the more. "You took me out of a ticklish situation tonight. I don't want any mere policemen to spoil my little game. Please oil up your forgettery with these, and then - forget!"

"Say, gov'nor," retorted the driver, as he put the money into the band of his leather cap. "I ain't seen so much real change since my boss got stung on the war. I ain't so certain but what you was the gink robbin' that house, at that. But that's them guys funeral if you beat 'em to it. Good-night - much obliged. But I got to slip it to you, gov'nor - you ain't none of them Central Office flat-feet, sure 'nuff! If you are a detective, you're some fly cop!"

CHAPTER IV

A SCIENTIFIC NOVELTY

In a private ward room at Bellevue Hospital, Captain Cronin was just returning to memory of himself and things that had been. Shirley arrived at his cot-side as he was being propped up more comfortably. The older man's face broke into game smiles, as the criminologist took the chair provided by the pretty nurse.

"Thanks, I'll have a little chat with my friend, if you don't think it will do him any harm."

"He is better now, sir. We feared he was fatally injured when they brought him in. I'll be outside in the corridor if you need anything."

She left not without an admiring look at the big chap, wondering why he wore such disreputable superstructure with patent leather pumps and silk hose showing below the ragged overcoat. Strange sights come to hospitals, curiosity frequently leading to unprofitable knowledge: so she was silently discreet. Shirley's garb was not unobserved by the detective chief. Monty laughed reminiscently at the questioning glance.

"These are my working clothes - a fine combination. I nabbed two of the gang. But what became of you?"

"Outside that club door, I wanted to save time for us both. I took the first taxi in sight. Before I could even call out to you, the door slammed on me, the shades flopped down, the car started up - the next thing I knew this here nurse was sticking a spoon in my mouth, a-saying: 'Take this - it's fine for what ails you!'"

"I wonder if it could have been the same machine they left at Van Cleft's? I will tell you how things progressed." So he did, leaving out only the confidence of Professor MacDonald. The Captain became feverishly excited, until Shirley abjured him to beware of a relapse. "You must be calm, for the next twenty-four hours: there will be much for you to do, even then. Meanwhile, let me call up your agency; then you give them instructions over this table telephone to let Howard Van Cleft interview the little chorus girl, with his friend. I'll be the friend."

"I'm afraid I'm going to be snowed under in this case, Monty. The finest job I've had these dozen years. But you're square, and will do all you can."

"Old friend, I'll do what I can to make Van Cleft and the newspapers sure that you are the most wonderful sleuth inside or outside the public library. Here's your office - speak up. Let me lift you."

"Hello Pat!" called Cronin, as his superintendent came to the 'phone. "I am detained at Bellevue, so that I can't be there when Van Cleft comes down. Let him Third Degree that little Jane from the garage. Keep them two men apart, too - oh, that's all right, the fellow is a friend of mine on the 'Frisco police force. He won't butt in." Silence for a moment, then: "Oh, shucks, let 'em yowl! They've got more than kidnapping to worry about for the next twenty-five years."

He hung up the receiver, sinking back on his pillows wan from the strain. Monty handed him a glass of water, and adjusted the bandages with a hand as tender as a woman's. He lifted the instrument again.

Eustace Hale Ball

"You are sterling, twenty-two carat and a yard wide, Captain! Now, get to sleep while I find out who the ring-master is. I've sworn to keep awake until I do. I think it well to telephone Van Cleft, and arrange for a better get-a-way for us both."

He was soon talking with the son of the murdered man. "Meet me down at the Vanderbilt Hotel - ask for Mr. Hepburn's room, and send up the name of Williams. See you in an hour. Good-bye."

Hanging up the receiver, he turned toward the door, after a friendly pat on Cronin's shoulder. The bell rang, and the Captain reached for it, to sink back exhausted upon the bed. Shirley answered, to be greeted by a pleasant feminine voice.

"Is this Captain Cronin?"

Instantly the criminologist replied affirmatively, suiting his tones as best he could to the gruff voice of the detective chief, with a wink at that worthy.

"I just called up, Captain, to ask about you - Oh, you don't recognize my voice. I'm Miss Wilberforce, private secretary to Mr. Van Cleft. Has any one been to see you yet? I understand that you are very busy, and have already missed two other good cases, this one being the THIRD! Well, don't hurry, Captain. You may get the rest to come - if you live long enough. Good-bye!"

Shirley looked at Cronin, startled. Another mention of the mystic number. He called for information about the origin of the call.

"Lordee, son! Are they at it again?" asked Cronin in disgust.

"Yes - overdoing it. One thing is clear, that whoever is behind this telephone trickery is very clever, and very conceited over that cleverness. It may be a costly vanity. Yes, information?"

"The call was from Rector 2190-D. The American Sunday School Organization, sir - It doesn't answer now; the office must be closed."

Shirley put the instrument down, with a smile on his pursed lips. He waved a good natured farewell to his friend, as he drew the cap down over his eyes.

"Look a little happier, Captain. I'll send down some fruit and a special vintage from our club which has bottled up in it the sunlight of a dozen years in Southern France. I hope they keep the telephone wires busy - they may tangle themselves up in their own spider-web!"

Leaving the hospital, he hurried to the hotel. One of his secret idiosyncracies was a custom of "living around" at a number of hotels, under aliases. Maintaining pleasant suites in each, he kept full supplies of linen and garments, while effectively blotting out his own identity for "doubling" work.

He was known as "Mr. Hepburn" here, and entering the side door he was subjected to the curious gaze of only one servant, the operator of the small elevator. Once in the shelter of his quarters he rummaged through some scrap-books for data - he found it in a Sunday feature story published a month before in a semi-theatrical paper. It described with rollicking sarcasm, a gay "millionaire" party which had been given in Rector's private dining rooms. Among the ridiculed hosts were Van Cleft, Wellington Serral and Herbert De Cleyster! Here, in some elusive manner, ran the skein of truth which if followed would lead to the solution of mystery. He must carve out of this mass of pregnant clues the essentials upon which to act, as the sculptor chisels the marble of a huge block to expose the figure of his inspiration, encased there all the time!

"To find out the source of their golden-haired nymphs for this merry-merry, that is the question! Some stage doorkeeper might be persuaded to unburden what soul he has left!"

He jotted in his memorandum book the names of the other eight wealthy men who were pilloried by the journalist. The younger men, Shirley felt sure, were of that peculiarly Manhattanse type of hanger-on - well-groomed, happy-go-hellward youths who danced, laughed and drank well, - so essential to the philanderings of these rich old Harlequins and their gilded Columbines. As he scribbled, the telephone of the room tinkled its summons.

He started toward it: then his invaluable intuition prompted him to walk into the adjoining room, where another instrument stood on a small table, handy to the bed. Only two people could possibly know he was there. Van Cleft could not have arrived, as yet. The other bell jingled impatiently, but Shirley finally heard the voice of the switch-board girl.

"I'm trying to get you on the other wire, sir. There's a call."

"Don't connect me," he hurriedly ordered, "except to open the switch, so I may listen. If I hang up without a word, tell the party I will be back in twenty minutes."

With a hotel telephone girl tact is more important than even the knowledge of wire-knitting. It was the woman's voice which he had heard at the hospital. Captain Cronin was anxious to speak to Mr. Williams, who was calling on Mr. Hepburn! With the biggest jolt of this day of surprises Shirley disconnected and whistled. Again he laughed - with that grim chuckle which was so characteristic of his supreme battling mood! They had found the trail even quicker than he had expected. Fortunate it was that he had not mentioned his own name in telephoning from the hospital to Howard. Not a wire was safe from these mysterious eaves-droppers now. He hurried into a business suit, and left the hotel, to walk over Thirty-fourth Street to the studio of his friend, Hammond Bell. Here he was admitted, to find the portrait-painter finishing a solitary chafing-dish supper.

"Delighted, Monty! Join me in the encore on this creamed

chicken and mushrooms!"

"Too rich for my primitive blood, Hammond. I'm in a hurry to get a favor."

"I've received enough at your hands - say the word."

"Simply this: I want to experiment with sound waves. I remembered that once in a while some of these wild Bohemian friends of yours warbled post-impressionist love-songs into your phonograph. It stood the strain, and so must be a good one. It is too late now to get one in a shop; will you lend me the whole outfit, with the recording attachment as well, for to-night and to-morrow?"

"The easiest thing you know. Let's slide it into this grip - you can carry the horn."

Three minutes later Shirley made his exit, and soon was shaking hands with Van Cleft in his own room at the hotel. He sketched his idea hurriedly, as he adjusted the instrument on the dressing-table near the telephone.

"When the call comes, be sure to say: 'Get closer, I can't hear you.' That's the method, and it's so simple it is almost silly." They were barely ready when the bell warned them. At Van Cleft's reply, when the call for "Mr. Williams" Shirley pushed the horn close to the telephone receiver. Van Cleft twisted it, so as to give the best advantage, and demanded that the speaker come closer to the 'phone.

"Can you hear me now?" asked the feminine voice. "Do you hear me now?"

"No, speak louder. This is Mr. Williams. Speak up. I can't understand you." The voice was petulant and so distinct that even Shirley could hear it, as he knelt by the side of the phonograph. Again Van Cleft insisted on his deafness. There was the suggestion of a break in the voice which brought to

Shirley's eyes the sparkle of a presentiment of success. At last Van Cleft admitted that he could hear.

"Well, you fool, I've a message for your friend Mr. Van Cleft."

"Which one?" was the innocent inquiry, as he forgot for an instant that now he was the sole bearer of that name.

"The one that's left. Tell him there will be none left if he continues this gum-shoe work. He had better let well enough alone, and let that little girl get out of town as soon as possible. The papers will go crazy over a scandal like this, and some one is apt to grab Van Cleft. That's all. Good-bye!"

Silently Shirley shut off the lever of the machine, to catch up the receiver. As before his endeavor to locate the call resulted in a new address: this time in the Bronx!

"Ah, the lady leaps from the business district to the Bronx in half an hour. That is what I call some traveling."

Van Cleft studied him with open mouth, as he withdrew the phonograph record, coating it with the preservative to make the tiny lines permanent.

"In the name of common sense, who was that? And what's this phonograph game?" he demanded.

"The second question may answer the first before sunrise, unless I am badly mistaken. I have heard an old adage which declares that if you give a man long enough rope he will hang himself. My new application is that you let him talk enough he is apt to sing his own swan song, for a farewell perch on the electric chair at Sing Sing!"

Then he lit a cigarette and packed up the phonograph.

CHAPTER V

THE MISBEHAVIOR OF THE 'PHONE

Still befuddled by the unusual events of the day, Howard Van Cleft was unable to delight in a theoretical discovery. Personal fear began to manifest itself.

"Mr. Shirley, you're going at this too strong. We know the guilty party - this miserable girl in the machine. We want to hush it up and let things go at that."

"We're hushing it, aren't we?" demanded Shirley, as he placed the record in the grip. "Don't you see the wisdom of knowing who may systematically blackmail you after secrecy is obtained. This is a matter of the future, as well as the present."

"But I don't want to lose my own life - I am young, with life before me, and I want to let well enough alone, after these threats."

"I am afraid that you have a yellow streak." His lip curled as he studied the pallid features of the heir to the Van Cleft millions. Fearless himself, he could still understand the tremors of this care-free butterfly: yet he knew he must crush the dangerous thoughts which were developing. "If you mistrust me, hustle for yourself. You have the death-certificate, the services will be over in a few days, and then you will have enough money to live on your father's yacht or terra firma for the rest of your life, in the China Sea, or India, as far away from Broadway chorus girls as you want. That might be safe."

He gazed out of the window, toward the twinkling lights far away across the East River. His sarcasm made Van Cleft wince as though from a whip lash. The latter mopped his forehead and tried to steady his voice, as he replied with all humility.

"You're a brick, and I don't mean to offend you. Today has been terrible, you know: this tornado has swept me from my moorings. I don't know where to turn."

"I am thoughtless," and Shirley's warm hand grasped the flaccid fingers of the young man. "Forgive me for letting my interest run away with my sympathies. I'm thinking of the future, more than mere protection from newspaper scandal. This crime is so ingenious that I believe it has a more powerful motive than mere robbery. You are now at the head of a great house of finance and society. You must guard your mother and your sister, and those yet to come. A deadly snake is writhing its slimy trail somewhere: here - there - 'round about us! Who knows where it will strike next? Who knows how far that blow may reach - even unto China, or wherever you run?"

He hesitated, studying the effect upon Van Cleft, who dropped limply into a chair, his eyes dark with terror. The Psychological ruse had won. Selfish cowardice, which temporarily threatened to ruin his campaign, now gave way to the instinct of a fighting defense.

"There, Van Cleft, it is ghastly. You have the significance now: we must scotch the snake. That girl is over at the Holland Agency, and we should see her at once, to learn what she knows. Cronin has arranged for my coming with you, so introduce me under my real name.

"Wait here fifteen minutes after I leave, so that I may get the phonograph in readiness, for you will undoubtedly be shadowed, and that may mean another telephone call. You were not a coward in college - I do not believe you are one now!"

Van Cleft straightened up proudly.

"No, I will fight them with all I have. But why these phonograph records: isn't one enough?"

"No, I want autographs of all the voices. I will go now. Don't hurry in following me. Do not fear to let any shadowers see you - it will help us along."

Before many minutes he had been admitted to the corridor of the Holland Agency by a sharp-nosed individual who regarded him with suspicion. The operatives were undoubtedly expecting trouble from all quarters, for three other large men of the "bull" type, heavy-jowled, ponderous men, surrounded him as he presented his card.

"I am the friend of Howard Van Cleft, about whom Captain Cronin telephoned you from Bellevue. I am to help him interview the girl: may I wait until he arrives?"

"Oh, you're wise to the case? Sure then, come into the reception room on the right. What's that in your grip?" asked the apparent leader of the men.

"Just an idea of Van Cleft's," said Shirley, as he followed into the adjoining compartment. "It's a phonograph. Have you received any phoney 'phone calls to-night? Queer ones that you didn't expect and couldn't explain? Van Cleft has, and he decided to take records of them on this machine."

The superintendent nodded. Shirley opened the grip and drew out the instrument, and made ready on the small table, near which was the desk telephone.

"Let's get this in readiness then, and if you get any calls have them switched up to this instrument, so that when you talk, you can hold the receiver handy to the horn."

"Young feller, I think you must know more about this business than you've a right to. Just keep your hands above the table - I think I'll frisk you!"

"No need," snapped Shirley with a smile in his eyes, and the automatic revolver was drawn and covering the detective before he could reach forward. "But I have no designs on you. You will have to work quicker than that with some people in this case."

He slid the weapon across the table to the other who snatched it anxiously.

"If a call comes and you don't recognize the voice at once, please ask the party to come closer to the 'phone, to speak louder - listen, there is the bell now! Get it connected here at once!"

The surprised superintendent, fearing that after all he might miss some good lead, yielded to his professional curiosity against his professional prejudices. He bawled down the hall.

"Switch on up here, Mike. I'll talk." He caught up the instrument, as Shirley dropped to his knees beside him, to swing the horn into place.

"What's that?" he shouted over the wire. "Yes, shure it is - What's that you say? - I don't get you, cull - You want to speak to the girl? - What girl? - Talk louder. Hire a hall! - Say, I ain't no mind reader! Speak up."

Over the instrument came the phrase once more: "Can you hear me now?"

It was the man's voice! Shirley was exultant.

"Yes, I hear you. What do you want?"

"I want to call for my sister, if you're going to let her go. I want - "

An inspiration prompted Shirley to press down the prongs of the receiver. The connection was stopped, and the superintendent turned upon him angrily.

"You spoiled that, you nut! We was just about to find out who her brother was - say, who are you, anyway?"

"There, don't you worry. That makes another call certain. Don't you see? That's what I'm playing for. But here comes Van Cleft, who will tell you I am all right."

The millionaire entered the hallway before any serious altercation could arise. He greeted Shirley warmly and introduced him to Pat Cleary. The man was mollified.

"Well, I'm Captain Cronin's right bower, and I thinks as how this guy is the joker of the deck trying to make a dirty deuce out of me. But, if you want to see the girl, she's right upstairs. His work was a little speedy on first acquaintance. Nick, keep your eyes on this machine, for we may get another call on this floor - This way gentlemen. Watch your step, for the hallway's dark."

The girl was imprisoned in a windowless room on the second floor. As the door opened, Shirley beheld a pitiful sight. Attired in the finery of the Rialto, she lay prone upon a couch in the center of the dingy room, sobbing hysterically. Her blonde hair was disheveled, her features wan and distorted from her paroxysms of fear and grief. Like a frightened animal, she sprang to her feet as they entered the room, retreating to the wall, her trembling hands spread as though to brace her from falling.

"I didn't do it! I swear! The old fool was soused and I don't know what was the matter with me. But I didn't kill any one in the world!"

"There, sit down, little girl, and don't get frightened. This gentleman and I have come to learn the truth - not to punish you for something you didn't do. Start with the beginning and tell all you remember."

Shirley's gentle manner was so unexpected, his voice so inspiring that she relaxed, sinking to the floor, as Shirley caught her limp girlish form in his arms. He placed her on the couch again, and she regained her composure under his calm urging. Little by little she visualized the details of the gruesome evening and narrated them under the magnetic cross-questions of the criminologist.

She had met the elder Van Cleft in the tea-room of a Broadway hostelry, by appointment made the evening before at Pinkie Taylor's birthday party. After several drinks together they took a taxicab to ride uptown to a little chop house. Did she see any one she knew in the tea-room? Of course, several of the fellows and girls whom she couldn't remember just now, buzzed about, for Van Cleft was a liberal entertainer around the youngsters. She had five varieties of cocktails in succession, and she became dizzy. In the taxicab she became dizzier and when next she remembered anything definite she was sitting on the stool in the garage where she had been arrested. That was all. As she reached this point there came a knock on the door with a call for Van Cleft.

"You Van's son!" she screamed. Then she fainted, while Shirley caught her, calling an assistant to care for her, as he followed Van Cleft downstairs to answer the telephone. "You know your cues?"

The millionaire nodded, as with trembling fingers he caught up the instrument and knelt on the bare floor to hold it close to the phonograph, which Shirley was engineering, with a fresh record in place.

"Hello! Hello, there, I say. Hello!"

Shirley strained his ears, to hear this time a rough, wheezy voice which caused the two men to exchange startled glances, as it proceeded: "Is this you, Howard, my boy?"

"What do you want? I can't hear you. The telephone is buzzing. Louder please!"

Shirley nodded approbation, as the machine ran along merrily.

"Now, can you hear me. Ahem! Can you hear me now? Is this Howard Van Cleft?"

"Yes, go ahead, but louder still."

"Now, can you hear me? This is your father's dearest friend, Howard, - this is William Grimsby speaking. I am fearfully distressed and shocked to learn of his death, my poor boy. And Howard, I am grieved to learn that there is some little scandal about it. As your father's confidential adviser, I urge you to hush it up at all cost. I was told at your home just now by one of the servants that you had gone to this vulgar detective agency."

Here Shirley shut off the phonograph, addressing Van Cleft with his hand over the mouthpiece of the telephone for the minute.

"Keep on talking until I return. Get his advice about flowers and everything else you can think of."

Then he ran from the room, into the hallway, out of the door, and down the stoop to Fortieth Street. He looked about uncertainly, then espied across the way a tailor shop, where the light of the late workman still burned. Monty hurried thither and asked the use of the telephone upon the wall.

"Shuair, mister, but it will cost you a dime, for I have to pay the gas and the rent."

Eustace Hale Ball

From the telephone directory he obtained the address and number of William Grimsby, the banker. He received an answer promptly. The servant, after learning his name promised to call the master. A gruff voice answered soon. Mr. Grimsby declared that he had been reading in his library for the last two hours, undisturbed by any telephone calls. Shirley expressed a doubt.

"How dare you doubt my word, sir. The telephone is in my reception room where I heard it ring just now, for the first time. What do you want?"

"An interview with you to-morrow morning at nine on a life and death matter. I can merely remind you, sir, that two of your friends, Wellington Serral and Herbert de Cleyster have met mysterious deaths during the past week. Mr. Van Cleft died of heart failure to-night. I will be there at nine. As you value your own life do not leave your residence or even answer any telephone messages again until I see you."

"Well, I'll be - " Shirley disconnected, before the verb was reached. He tossed the coin to the tailor, and speedily returned to the waiting room where he signaled Van Cleft to end the conversation.

"Quick now, find out what wire called you up." The answer was "William Grimsby, 97 Fifth Avenue."

"You had the wrong tip that time, Mr. Shirley," said Van Cleft. "But how could he have found out where I was, for none of the servants know about Captain Cronin, or even my family that I was coming down here. He gave me some good advice however. I want to pay the hush money and end it all forever."

Shirley had preserved the record and put it away with the others in the grip. Now he lit a cigarette and puffed several rings of smoke before answering.

"Van, it must be wonderful to be twins."

"This is no night for joking," petulantly, observed the nervous young man. "I want the girl silenced - "

"She won't open her mouth after I tell her some things. It may entertain you to know, Van, that while you were getting such good advice from Mr. Grimsby on this wire, I was talking to the real Mr. Grimsby on his own wire: he said I was his first caller in more than an hour. So, I gave him some good advice, which wouldn't interest you. After this don't believe what the telephone tells."

"Who was I speaking with?"

"The most brilliant criminal it has ever been my pleasure to run across," and his eyes snapped with joy, the huntsman instinct rising to the surface at last, "I will call him the voice until I know his better name. He is the most scientific crook of the age."

"What do you know about criminals?" was the incredulous question.

"I'll know a hundred times as much as I do now, when I know all about this one, Van. You'd better have Cleary send an armed guard along with you, and get home for a good rest. Get a man who can drive a car, and bring back the empty auto three houses away from your residence: it will bear looking into! I'm going up to have a revival meeting with that girl now, for I am convinced that she is not a whit more implicated in the conception or execution of this crime than you are. Good-night."

Van Cleft left the house, with a pitying shake of the head. He was not quite certain that he had done wisely, after all, in bringing his eccentric friend into the affair. He little reckoned how much more peculiarly Montague Shirley was to act for the remainder of the night.

CHAPTER VI

AN EXPERIMENT WITH THE "MOVIES"

The cross-examination of Polly Marion resulted in little advantage. She had known of the sudden departure of two other songbirds, well equipped with funds for the land of Somewhere Else. Their absence had been the subject of some quiet jesting among the dragon flies who flitted over the pond of pleasure. A suggestion, from some unrecalled source, that their disappearance had been connected with the deaths of the two aged suitors was revitalized in her memory by the words of the elderly detective. Familiar with the strange life of this jeweled half-world Shirley's keenness brought forth nothing to convince him that the girl had been more culpable than in the following of her class, known to the initiate as the "gentle art of gold digging."

"Polly, go home now, and stay away from these parties: that's my honest advice, if you want to be on the 'outside looking in,' when some one is sent to prison for this. I am in favor of hushing up this affair, and want to ease it up for you. Are you wise?"

Polly was wise, beyond her years. Her equipoise was regained, and with a coquettish interest in this handsome interviewer - such girls always have an eye for future business - he returned to her theatrical lodging house, in which at least dwelt her wardrobe and makeup box when she was "trouping" in some spangled chorus. Of recent months she had not been subjected to the Hurculean rigors of bearing the spear, thanks to the gratuities of the open-handed Van Cleft, Senior. She pleaded to remain out of the white lights, meaning it as she spoke. But Shirley wisely felt that the butterfly would emerge from the chrysalis, shortly, to flutter into certain gardens where he would fain cull rare blossoms! Pat Cleary deputized a "shadow" to diarize her exits and entrances.

"The hooks are cleaned, with fresh bait upon them," soliloquized Shirley, as he went down the dark stoop. "Now for a little laboratory work on the wherefore of the why!"

Although long after midnight, he numbered among his acquaintanceship, many whom he could find far from Slumber-land. His steps led to the apartment of a certain theatrical manager, whom he found engaged in a lively tournament of the chips, jousting with two leading men, one playwright, a composer and a merchant prince. The latter, of course, was winning. The host, contributing both chips and bottled cheer, was far from optimistic until the arrival of the club man.

"A live one abaft the mizzen!" exclaimed Dick Holloway, "Here's Shirley sent by Heaven to join us. After all I hope to pay my next month's rent."

Noisily welcomed by the victims of mercantile prowess, he apologetically declined to flirt with Dame Fortune, pleading a business purpose.

"Business, Monty! By the shade of Shakspeare! I never knew you to look at business, except to prevent it running you down like a Fourth Avenue mail bus."

"It is in the interest of science," said Shirley, drawing the manager aside, "an experiment - "

"Fudge on science. You interrupt a game at this time of night!"

"But it means money. I am willing to pay."

"Ah, Monty, money should never come between friends, and so I retract: with three failures this season, because the public doesn't appreciate art."

"It's about moving pictures. I know that you have floated a syndicate for big productions. Do you work night and day?"

"An investment? Heaven bless you! Come into my bedroom and we'll arrange things of course, we work at night. Just this minute they are producing the 'Bartered Bride' in six reels and eighteen thrills a foot. A magnificently equipped studio, the public yelling for more how much have you?"

"Not so fast, Dick. It's merely some special work tonight, what you would call trick photography. I need a photographer, some lights, a little space, a microscopic lens and the complete developing during the night. And, I'll pay cash, as I have done with some suspicious poker losses in this temple of the muses on bygone evenings. Which, I may urge with gentle sarcasm is more than I have frequently received at your hands."

"Touche!" laughed Holloway. "I'll write a note to the studio manager - he's there now, and will do what you want. You could have your picture completed by morning with a little financial coaxing applied in the right place. Come to the library table. Go on with the game, boys, it will save me a little."

The potentate of dry goods was drawing in his winnings, as Shirley leaned over Holloway's shoulder to dictate the missive. Suddenly a revolver shot rang out from the window, and a bullet crashed into the wall behind Shirley's head.

His hand, idly dropped into his overcoat pocket, intuitively closed around his automatic revolver. A dark silhouette was outlined against the gray luminosity cast up by the lights of Broadway, half a block from the window. Through the opening another belching flame shot forth, to be answered by the criminologist's weapon, barking like a miltraileuse. They heard a stifled cry, and as Shirley ran forward, he exclaimed with disappointment.

"He's escaped down the fire-escape and through that skylight."

He faced about to smile grimly at the curious scene within. The playwright had taken refuge among the brass andirons of the big empty fireplace. The matinee heroes were under chairs, and Holloway behind the mahogany buffet. From the direction of the stairway came shrill cries from the speeding merchant, softening in intensity as he neared the street level.

"The battle's over!" exclaimed Holloway. "I don't know whether it was my chorus men wishing the gipsy curse on me, or the stage-carpenters going on a strike. But look! See the swag that Jerry left behind! What shall we do with it?"

"Loot!" suggested the playwright, with rare discrimination, as he dusted off the wood ashes, and approached the table with glistening eyes. "We'll divide share and share alike. It's the only way to win from Jerry."

Temperament was asserting its gameness. Shirley put back into position a shattered portrait of Sarah Bernhardt, and his eyes twinkled as the apostles of the muses hastened to divide the chips of the departed one into five generous piles. Holloway completed the letter, albeit with a nervous chirography, and handed him the envelope.

"Go now, before a submarine war zone is declared. I'm going to close up shop before the police come visiting. Good luck, Monty, in the cause of science."

Although his conscience was clear about the game having created five surprised winners by his interruption, he was disturbed over the certainty that the voice was aware of his personal work in the case. The difficulties were now trebled!

Eustace Hale Ball

Before any policemen appeared Shirley had passed Broadway on his way to the motion picture studio, on the West side of Tenth Avenue. Whatever secret observers may have been on his tracks, nothing untoward occurred: still, his senses were quickened into caution by the attempt on his life.

A parley with a grumpy gateman, the presentation of his letter and he was admitted to the presence of the manager, a man exhausted with the strenuosity of night and day work. Shirley understood the antidote for his sullenness.

"Here, old man, send out for a little luncheon for the two of us. I have some unusual experimental work, and need the assistance of a well-known expert like yourself." The flattery, embellished by a ten-dollar bill, opened a flood-gate of optimism.

A camera man was summoned, and the apparatus prepared for some "close-up" motion pictures. Under the weird green lights of the mercury vapor lamps, a director and company of players were busily enacting a dramatic scene, before a studio set. They gave little heed to the newcomer: boredom is a prime requisite of poise in the motion picture art.

"I have here three phonograph records, which I want photographed."

"But they don't move - you want a still camera," exclaimed the dumfounded manager.

"Yes, they do move as the picture is taken. I want a microscopic lens used in the camera in such a way that we take a motion picture of the twinings and twistings of one little thread on the wax cylinder, as it records the sound waves around the cylinder."

The photographer sniffed with scorn, being familiar with eccentric uplifters of the "movies," but responded to the command of the manager to adjust his delicate camera mechanism for the task.

"There is a certain phrase of words on each cylinder which I want recorded this way. Can all three be taken parallel with each other on the same film?"

"Sure, easiest thing to do - just a triple exposure. We take it on one edge of the film, through a little slit just a bit wider than the space of the thread, cut in a screen. Then we rewind that film, and slide the slit to the middle of the lens, take your second wax record, and do the same on the right edge of the film for the third. But what's the idea?"

The camera man began to show interest: he was a skilled mechanician and he caught the drift of a sensible purpose, at last.

Shirley did not answer. He placed the first record in the phonograph, running it until the feminine voice could be distinguished asking: "Can you hear me now?" He marked the beginning and end of this phrase with his pocket knife. So with the merry masculine and the aged, disagreeable voice, he located the same order of words: "Can you hear me now?" The operation seems easy, in the telling, or again perhaps it appears intensely involved and hardly worth the trouble. A motto of Shirley's was: "Nothing is too much trouble if it's worth while." So, with this. To the cynical camera man its general nature was expressed in his whispered phrase to the manager:

"You better not leave them property butcher knives on that there table, Mr. Harrison. This gink is nuts: he thinks's he's Mike Angelo or some other sculpture. He'll start sculpin' the crowd in a minute!"

"You take the picture and keep your opinions to yourself," snapped Shirley whose hearing was highly trained.

The man lapsed into silence. For two hours they fumed and perspired and swore, under the intense heat of the low-hung mercury lamps, until at last a test proved they had the right combination. Shirley greased the skill of the camera man with a well-directed gratuity, and ordered speedy development of the film. Before this was done, however, he took six other records of voices from the folk in the studio, using the same words: "Can you hear me now?"

The three strips of triple exposures were taken to the dark room and developed by the camera man. They were dried on the revolving electric drums, near a battery of fans. Shirley studied every step of the work, with this and that question - this had been his method of acquiring a curiously catholic knowledge of scientific methods since leaving the university, where sporting proclivities had prompted him to slide through courses with as little toil as possible.

A print upon "positive" film was made from each: every strip was duplicated twenty-five times, at Shirley's suggestion. Then after two hours of effort the material was ready to be run through the projecting machine, for viewing upon the screen.

The manager led Shirley to the small exhibition theatre in which every film was studied, changed and cut from twenty to fifty times before being released for the theatres. The camera man went into the little fire-proof booth, to operate the machine.

"Which one first, chief?"

"Take one by chance," said Shirley, "and I will guess its number. Start away."

There was a flare of light upon the screen, as the operator fussed with the lamp for better lumination. He slowly began to turn the crank, and the criminologist watched the screen with no little excitement. The picture thrown up resembled nothing so much as three endless snakes twisting in the same general rhythm from top to bottom of the frame. The twenty-five duplicates were all joined to the original, so that there was ample opportunity to compare the movements.

"Well, gov'nor, which film was that?" asked the operator.

"Not A - it was B or C!"

"Correct. How'd you guess it? Which is this one?"

As he adjusted another roll of film in the projector, Shirley turned to the manager sitting at his side. "Mr. Harrison, were those snakes all exactly alike?"

"No. They all wriggled in the same direction, at the same time. But little rough angles in some movements and queer curves in others made each individually different."

"Just what I thought. There goes another. - That is not film A, either!"

"Righto!" confirmed the camera man. As the detailed divergence between the lines became more evident in the repetitions, Shirley slapped his knee.

"Now for the finish. Try reel A."

This time the three snakey lines moved along in almost identical synchronism. The only difference was that the first was thin, the second heavier, the third the darkest and most ragged of all. The relationship was unmistakable!

"I got you gov'nor," cried the operator. "Some dope, all right, all right."

"Why, what is all this?" asked the manager, nonplussed. "The last three are alike, but what good does it do?"

"It is known that the human voice in its inflections is like handwriting - with a distinct personality. Certain words, when pronounced naturally, without the alterations of dialect, are always in the same rhythm. The records taken in the studio of those five words, 'Can you hear me now?' are in the same general rhythm, but only the last three snakes show exact similarity, to each little quaver and turn. There was only the difference in shading: one was the voice of a women. The second of a man of perhaps forty, the third of an old man - all three taken at different times, and I thought from different people. But they all came from one throat, and my work is completed along this line - Will you please lock up the films, the phonograph, and my records in your film vault, until I send for them; through Mr. Holloway?"

The criminologist arose and walked into the deserted studio, from whence the company had long since departed for belated slumbers. He picked up three bricks which lay in a corner of the big studio, and placed them gently into his grip. The manager and the camera man observed this with blank amazement, as he locked it and put the key into his pocket. Then he handed each of them a large-sized bill.

"I'm very grateful, gentlemen, for your assistance. Pleasant dreams."

Shirley abstractedly walked out of the studio, one hand comfortably in his overcoat pocket, swinging the grip in the other.

"Say, Lou," confided the manager, "he's the craziest guy I've ever seen in the movies. And that's going some, after ten years of it."

Lou treated himself to a generous bite of plug tobacco, and spat philosophically, before replying.

"Sure, he's crazy. Crazy, like the grandfather of all foxes!"

CHAPTER VII

ENTER A BEAUTIFUL WOMAN

A reddening zone in the East silhouetted the serrated line of the distant elevated structure, as Shirley walked along the gray street, his thoughts busy with the possibilities of applying his new certainty.

He had reached Sixth Avenue, and was just passing one of the elevated pillars when a black touring car crept up behind him. The clanging bell and the grinding motors of an early surface car drowned the sound of the automobile in his rear. Suddenly the big machine sprang forward at highest speed. A man leaned from the driver's seat, and snatched the grip from his hand.

The motorman, cursing, threw on the emergency brake, in time to barely graze the machine with his fender as it shot across the street before him.

Shirley's view was cut off, until he had run around the street-car - then he beheld the big automobile skidding in a half-circle, as it turned down Fifth Avenue. It was too far away to distinguish the number of the singing license tag.

"Much good may the bricks do them! Perhaps they will help to build the annex necessary up the river, when these gentry go there for a long visit."

Eustace Hale Ball

Shirley laughed at the joke on his pursuers, and turned into a little all-night grill for a comforting mutton chop of gargantuan proportions, with an equally huge baked potato. He was a healthy brute, after all his morbid line of activities! Later, at the Club, he submitted to the amenities of the barber, whose fine Italian hand smoothed away, in a skilful massage, the haggard lines of his long vigil. As he left the club house for William Grimsby's residence he looked as fresh and bouyant as though he had enjoyed the conventional eight hours' sleep.

"You are this Montague Shirley?" was the querulous greeting from the old gentleman, when he was admitted to the drawing-room. "You kept me in anguish the entire night, with your silly words. The telephone bell rang at intervals of half an hour until dawn: I may have missed some important business deal by not replying What do you mean? Is this some blackmail game?"

"No, sir. It has to deal with blackmailing, however - but not for my profit."

"Explain quickly. I am a busy man. My motor is waiting now to take me to my office."

"Look here, Mr. Grimsby, at this memorandum book," said Shirley, holding forward the list which he had copied from the joy-party article in the theatrical paper. "With some friends of yours, you held merry carnival to Venus and Bacchus at an all-night lobster palace not long ago. Have I the right names?"

"This is rank impertinence. How dare you? Get out of my house."

"Not so fast, my dear sir, until you understand my drift. Throughout Club circles you and Mr. Van Cleft, with these other cronies are sarcastically referred to as the Lobster Club. Did you know that?"

Grimsby's face was purple with angry mortification, but

Shirley would not be gainsaid. "I am acting in this matter as a friend of Howard Van Cleft," he continued. "Your three friends have met their deaths at the hand of a cunning conspirator. Last night, white I talked with you on the telephone, young Van Cleft was receiving advice over another wire from a person who pretended to be William Grimsby - advising him to hush the matter up and drop the investigation. But - Captain Cronin the famous detective - has received a tip that the number of victims would be increased very soon - frankly, now: do you want to be the fourth?"

Grimsby's face changed to ashen gray, as he timidly clutched Shirley's sleeve.

"Then cooperate with me. You understand now the nature of this villain's work: to rob and assassinate his victim in the company of a girl, so that this would endeavor to hush the scandal, without reporting it to the police. His progress is unchecked, and afterwards he would have untold opportunity for continuing a demand for hush money on the surviving relatives. May I count on you to help?"

"You may count on me to leave the city within the next two hours."

"Good! But I want to have you disappear so quietly that this cunning unknown will not know of it. He is watching your house now, without a doubt."

Grimsby strode to the window, with his characteristic limp, and drew the heavy curtains aside, to peer out nervously.

"No one is in sight."

"The man is as unseen in his work as a germ. But he is not unheard: he uses the telephone to locate his victims, that is why I advised you to let your instrument ring unanswered."

"I'll do what I can, if I can keep out of more danger. An old man craves life more than a young one. I fought through the Civil War and brought a medal from Congress and this wounded knee out of it, Mr. Shirley. I didn't fear anything then, but times have changed!"

"Here is my plan, then," continued Shirley, his lips twitching with sub-strata amusement, "I want to impersonate you, when you leave, so that this man tries to send me after the other three. Don't interrupt, let me finish - You will say that it is impossible to deceive any one at close range. Surely, it does sound melodramatic, like a lurid tale of a paper back novel. But I have studied the photographs of your friends. You and I bear the closest resemblance of any in the group. Your weight is about the same as mine - your shoulders are a trifle stooped and you walk with a curious drag of your left foot. Your hair is white but thick: the contour of our faces is quite similar, and so with dry cosmetics, some physical mimicry, and the use of a pair of horn-rimmed glasses like yours I can make a comparatively good double. The only exposure to the sharp eyes of your enemies will be, first, when I substitute myself for you and take your automobile back home; second, when I go down to the theatrical district, to visit a well-known tearoom where I learn you are a frequent guest. There the wall tables are shrouded by decorations, and I shall keep in the shadow and talk as little as possible. Behind those dark glasses, and entering the place with your peculiarly spotted fur coat, I will resemble you more than you believe. If to add to the illusion, I show hospitable prodigality with drinks for the others, it is probable that their observation will be less analytical. Then, third in the line of activities, I will go to the theatre, sit in a darkened box, and let them take me where they will in whatever automobile turns up. Thus you see my campaign."

"How much do I have to pay you?"

"I might have expected that," was the laughing retort. "You are noted for the fortunes you waste on stupid show girls, while times are hard with you in your offices where young and old men struggle along to support honest families. Have no fear,

Mr. Grimsby, my income is enough for my simple wants. I am entering this hunt for big game, just as I have gone to India and East Africa, for jungle trophies. It will not cost you a nickel."

"I had better contribute a little," began Grimsby, embarrassed, as he drew out a check-book. But Shirley negatived with emphasis.

"How about your servants? Can you trust them with the secret?"

"They have been with me for twenty-five years or more. My wife is in California, and the rest of the servants, except two maids and a butler, up at my country home on the Hudson."

"Fine: then, in two hours from now, meet me at the Hotel Astor, where I have rooms, in the name of Madden. Bring down an extra suit of clothes, and an extra overcoat, for I want to wear your fur one, which I see there on the davenport. On the downward trip instruct your chauffeur to drive your car up to your country place, as soon as he has made the return trip from the hotel. You will be there before he gets up, on the country roads and he will be none the wiser. Goodbye, Mr. Grimsby."

At the club Shirley made some necessary disposition of his private matters, for he knew this case would run longer than a day. From his rooms he sent a note by messenger to his theatrical friend, Dick Holloway, which read simply.

"Dear Holloway: - The experiment with the movies won the blue ribbon. I have a new plan on foot. You can help me in this, as well. I want you to engage for me a beautiful, clever and daring actress, afraid of nothing under the sun or moon, and absolutely unknown on Broadway. No amateurs or stage-struck heiresses or manicurists: you are the one impresario who can fill my bill. I will call at your office in fifteen minutes, so have the compact sealed by then. Who finally won the loot, last night?

Your friend, Montague Shirley."

The manager was forced to go through the note twice, to make sure that his senses were not leaving him. Then he turned in the chair, toward the unusual young woman who sat in his private office, observing with mingled amusement and curiosity the fleeting expressions upon his face.

"In view of your mission in America, this may interest you," was his amused comment, as he handed her the missive. "It is from the most curious man in New York."

He studied the downcast lashes, as she read the letter. Hers was a face which had stirred a continent, yet he had never met her until this memorable day. She might have been twenty-three years old - and again, might have been three years younger or older. Rippling red-gold waves of hair separated in the center of her smooth brow to caress with a soft wave on either side the blooming cheeks, whose Nature-grown roses were unusual in this world-weary vicinity of Broadway. A sweet mouth with a sensuous smile at one corner, and a barely perceptible droop of pathos at the other, lent an indescribable piquance to her dimpled smile. The blue orbs which raised to his own with a Sphinxian laugh in their azure depths thrilled him - Holloway, the blase, the hardened theatrical manager, flattered and cajoled by hundreds of beautiful women on the quest of stage success!

Adroitly veiled beneath the silken folds of the clinging gown, redolent with the bizarre artistry of a Parisian atelier, was the shapely suggestion of exquisite physical perfection which did not escape the connoisseur glance of Holloway.

"He is a literary man: I know that from the small, yet fluent writing, and the cross marks for periods show that he has written for newspapers and corrected his own proofs - He is unusually definite in what he desires and accustomed to having his imperious way about most things. In this case, he is easily pleased - merely perfection is his desire."

"Shirley is generally prompt, and is apt to breeze in here any second now, with his two hundred pounds and six feet of brawn and ginger. I wonder - "

"Why do you suppose such a paragon is desired by your friend? Who is he? What is he like, not an ordinary actor - " and the wondrous eyes darkened with a curious thought.

"My dear lady, no one has discovered the mental secrets of Montague Shirley. He apparently wastes his life as do other popular society men with much money and more time on their hands. Yet, somehow, I always feel in his presence as one does when standing on the bow of an ocean liner, with the salt breeze whizzing into your heart. He is a force of nature, yet he explains nothing: a thorough man of the world; droll, sarcastic, generous and I believe for democracy he is unequaled by any Tammany politician: he knows more policemen, dopes, conductors, beggars, chauffeurs, gangsters, bartenders, jobless actors, painters, preachers, anarchists, and all the rest of New York's flotsam and jetsam than any one in the world. He is always the polished gentleman, and yet they take him man for man."

"What does this unusual person do for a living?"

"Nothing but living!"

Her interest was naturally undiminshed by this perfervid tribute, and she clapped her dainty hands together with sudden mirth.

"You know why I came here, and why to you, Mr. Holloway. You know who I am, and although I answer none of those exorbitant terms except that I am not known by sight along your big street Broadway, why not recommend me for the position?"

"But you, of all people!" Holloway's face was a study in amazement. "You can't tell what wild project he has in view. Shirley is a wild Indian, in many things you know - just when you least expect it. I have known him a dozen years."

He paused to weigh the matter, and his sense of humor conquered. He roared with mirth, which was joined in more sedately by the unknown girl. "That settles it. You couldn't start on your campaign in a better way. You shall be the Lady of Mystery in this story! I will not breathe a hint of your identity to Shirley, and no one else knows, of course. What a ripping good joke: I'm glad you came here the first hour after your landing in New York."

"What shall I call myself? I have it - a romantic name, which will be worth laughing over later - let me see - Helene Marigold. Is that flowery enough?"

"Shirley will be sure you are an actress when he hears that. Mum is the word, may you never have stage fright and never miss a cue - Here he comes now!"

The criminologist rushed into the office impetuously, dropping his bag on the floor, and doffing his hat as he beheld the pretty companion of Holloway.

"On time to the minute, as usual, Shirley. Your note came, and I followed your instructions. Let me present to you your new star, Miss Helene Marigold, who just disembarked on the steamer from England this morning. You have secured a young lady who is making all Europe sit up and rub its eyes. I believe I have at last found a match for you, Prince of the Unexpected!"

Shirley held forth his fervent hand, and was surprised at the almost masculine sincerity with which the delicately gloved fingers returned the pressure. He looked into the blue eyes with a challenging scrutiny, and received as frank an answer!

Dick Holloway indulged in an unobserved smile, as he turned to look out of the window, lost for the nonce in mirthful speculation.

CHAPTER VIII

WHEN GREEK MEETS GREEK

"Dick, you can help me further, with your dramatic knowledge. I feel in duty bound to tell Miss Marigold that she is risking her life, if she takes up this task."

Instead of hesitancy, which Shirley half expected, the girl's face flushed with quickened interest, and her eyes sparkled with enjoyment as he unfolded the situation. At the mention of Grimsby, Holloway grunted with disgust - it may have been a variety of professional jealousy. Who knows? However, the problem fascinated the mysterious young woman, who blushed, in spite of herself, when Shirley put his blunt question to her.

"And you are willing to assume for a time the character of one of these stage moths, whom rich men of this type pursue and woo, wine, dine and boast about? Will it interfere with your own work? Any salary arranged by Mr. Holloway is agreeable, for this unusual task."

"The game, not the money, is the attraction. I will be ready when you pronounce my cue."

"Splendid. Dick, will you assist Miss Marigold in selecting an attractive apartment in a theatrical hotel this afternoon. I will call for her at four-thirty, to take her to tea. She may not know me, at first glance: that depends upon the help you give me at the Astor. I will expect you there in an hour. I haven't acted since I left the college shows: with a hundred chances to one against my success, even I am not bored."

He hurried from the office, and Holloway noted the glow in the girl's glance which followed his stalwart figure. Holloway was a good tactician: there were reasons why he enjoyed this new role of match-maker de luxe, yet he played his hand far more subtly than at poker. Which was well!

Ensconced in the Astor, Shirley was soon busy before the cheval glass, from which were suspended three photographs of William Grimsby, obtained from a photographic news syndicate.

Coat and waistcoat had been removed, as he discriminatingly applied the dry cosmetics with skill which suggested that he had disguised himself for daylight purposes far more than he would admit. By the time he had powdered his thick locks with the white pulverized chalk, and donned a pair of horn-rim glasses of amber tint, his whole personality had changed. The similarity was startling to the prototype who was admitted to the room a few minutes later.

"Why, I beg pardon - I have come to the wrong suite," were Grimsby's apologetic words, as he essayed to retreat.

"You are the first victim of the mirage. Do you like the caricature?"

"Astounding, my friend!" gasped Grimsby, sinking into the chair. Shirley drew him to the mirror, to make a closer study of the lines of senility and late hours. A few delicate touches of purple and blue, some retouching of the nostrils, and he drew on the suit provided by his elder. Dick Holloway was announced, and Shirley ordered some wine and a dinner for one! At Grimsby's surprise, Shirley, smiled indulgently.

"I am selfish - I will have a little supper party by myself, and spare you in nothing. I want you to eat, to drink, to pour wine, to take out your wallet, to walk, to sit down, to laugh, to scold! You have a task, sir: I will imitate you move by move! This is a rare experiment."

"Great Scott! Which is you?" cried Holloway who entered with the burdened waiter.

"Neither. We're both me!" chuckled the criminologist. "But let me introduce you to my twin - "

The two men exchanged formalities with an undercurrent of dislike. Shirley lost no time. He compelled the old man to run through his paces, as Holloway criticized each study in miming. Just as the capitalist would swing his arms, limp with his left leg, shift his head ever so little, from side to side in his walk, so Shirley copied him. A word here, an exhortation there, and Shirley improved steadily under Holloway's analytical direction. At last the lesson was ended, with the manager's pronounciamento of "graduation cum lauda."

"I'll have to star you, Monty," he declared, as Shirley put on the fur greatcoat of the old man, grasping the gold headed cane, and drooping his shoulders in a perfect imitation of the other's attitude.

"Perhaps it will be necessary. The chorus men have invaded society with their fox-trots and maxixe steps. We club men will have to countercharge the enemy, for self-preservation, to play heavy villains upon the stage. Eh?"

He turned toward Grimsby, who was well wearied with the trying ordeal, and evidencing a growing nervousness about his own escape.

"You know how to leave, according to my plan? Wrap the muffler well around the lower part of your face, button this second overcoat closely about your neck, and enter the private carriage which I ordered for 'Mr. Lee,' waiting now at the

Forty-fifth Street Side. Then drive leisurely to the West Forty-second Street Ferry, where you can catch the late afternoon train for your country place."

"Good-bye, Mr. Shirley. I have been an old curmudgeon with you, I fear. You have taught this old dog new tricks in several ways, young man. Neither I nor my friends will forget your bravery. They are all out of the city by now, according to word from my private secretary. Your field is clear. Good luck, sir!"

Shirley and Holloway left the rooms first. Neither addressed the other on the lift, as it descended to the street level. Holloway casually followed Monty as he stiffly walked to the big red limousine waiting at the Forty-fourth Street entrance of the hostelry. The chauffeur sprang out, opening the door with a respectful salute. The disguise was successful!

"Home!" grunted Shirley, sinking back into the car, with collar high about his neck and the soft hat half concealing his eyes. He scrutinized the faces of the passers-by, photographing in that receptive memory of his the ugly features of two men, who peered into the limousine from under the visors of their black caps. The car sped up town through the bewildering maze of street traffic. The chauffeur helped him up the steps of the brownstone mansion, while Grimsby's old butler swung open the glass door, with a helping hand under the feeble arm.

Shirley puffed and grunted impatiently until he heard the door close behind him. Then straightening up, he turned upon the startled butler.

"Well, my man. Go out and tell the chauffeur to leave for the country at once, as Mr. Grimsby already ordered him to do."

"My Gawd, sir!" exclaimed the servant, paling perceptibly. "What's come over you, sir? - Oh, I beg pardon, sir, you're the other gentleman. You certainly fooled me, sir - You're bloody brave, sir, to do all this for the master. Are we in any danger?"

"Not a bit - whatever happens will be outside the house. Just keep up the secret, as you value your master's life. Go, and tell the man. I must kill time here in the library, reading until four o'clock."

Shirley threw aside the greatcoat, and walked to the window of the small reception room which faced the street, to draw aside the curtains and watch the chauffeur, as he entered the machine to speed away. A black automobile slowly passed the house, bearing two men on the driver's seat. From under the visors of their black caps they scrutinized the building, to hastily look away as they observed the face at the window.

Shirley made a note of the number of the machine. He could have sworn that this was the same car which had passed him that morning at dawn when the grip was snatched from his hand.

He returned to the library, where he lost himself in the rare old volumes of Grimsby's life collection: the criminologist was a booklover and the hours drifted by as in a happy playtime, until the butler came to tell him the time.

"Great Scott! I must hurry. Call a taxi, for me. I will go to Holloway's office to learn where Miss Marigold has been ensconced."

He sat in the machine before the office building, as he sent the chauffeur up to Dick's office, to inquire for a message to "Mr. Grimsby." A note was brought down, informing him that the girl awaited him in the Hotel California, a few blocks above. The machine started off once more, and Shirley laughed at the droll situation in which he found himself.

"I wonder who Helene Marigold can be? I wonder what Holloway meant precisely when he predicted that I would meet my match. I am not seeking one kind - and blue eyes, surrounded by red-gold hair and peaches and cream will not shake my determination."

But the best laid determinations of bachelor hearts gang aft agley!

Down at the Hotel California, famous for its rare collection of attractive feminine guests and the manifold breach-of-promise suits which had emanated from the palm bedecked entrance, Helene Marigold was indulging herself in a delighted, albeit highly amused, inspection of sundry large boxes which had been arriving from shops in the neighborhood.

"As nearly as I can imagine this must look like the bower of a Broadway Phryne. All that is missing is a family portrait in crayon of the father who was a coal miner, the presence of a buxom financial genius for the stage mother, and a Chinese chow-dog on a cerise velvet cushion. But who ever attains perfection here below?"

She lifted some filmy gowns which had arrived in the latest parcel to her chin, peering over the sheerness of the lacy cascade, into the mirror of the dressing-table.

"If good old Jack could see me now? Poor, old, stupid, dear, silly Jack! I must write to him at once, for he is largely responsible for my present unusual surroundings. How pleased this would not make him, the old dear."

With the thought, she sat down before the escritoire, dipping a pearl and gold pen, as she paused for the words with which to begin the note. Another knock came at the door. It could not be another gown. She had told Holloway to keep all her personal baggage at the steamer dock until she had finished her lark! At the portal a diminutive messenger delivered a large white box, ornately bound in lavender ribbons. When she unwrapped it, hidden in the folds of many reams of delicate tissue, she found a gorgeous bunch of orchids.

"How beautiful! I wonder who could have - " then she found a white card, and read it aloud, with a mirthful peal of laughter.

"To Lollypop's little Bonbon Tootems - from her foolish old Da-Da!"

Helene turned toward the window, to gaze out over the mysterious, foreign motley array of roofs and obtruding skyscrapers of this curious district.

"This mysterious man plays his part with a sense of humor. If only he will be different and not mean the flowers, ever!"

And she forgot to finish the note which was to have gone to faraway, stupid, dear old Jack.

Ten minutes later an aged gentleman entered the gorgeous foyer of the Hotel California, impatiently presenting his card to the bell-boy, for announcement to Miss Marigold. The lad, true to tradition, quietly confided the name to the interested clerk, before doing so. As the visitor was shown to the elevator, the clerk turned to his assistant with a nudge.

"There's the easiest spender of the Lobster Club. That means good trade here, with this new peach in the crate. These old ginks are hard as Bessemer armor-plate in business, but oh, how soft the tumble for a new shade of peroxide."

"Mr. Grimsby" was soon sitting on the velour divan, at a comfortable distance from possible eavesdroppers at the door. She was putting the finishing touches to her preparation for the butterfly role. Shirley felt an unexpected thrill at this little intimacy of their relations: the rooms were permeated with the most delicate suggestion of a curious perfume, which was strange to him. Somehow it fitted her personality so effectually: for despite the physical appeal of her beauty, now accentuated by the risque costume which she had donned, at the professional suggestion of Dick Holloway, there was a pervasive spirituality in the girl's face, her hands, and the tones of her soft voice.

She turned to smile at him, her dimples playing hide and seek with the white pearls beneath the unduly scarlet lip.

"Isn't this a ripping good situation for a novel?" she began.

"Yes, too good at present, Miss Marigold. There are too many, important people to be affected for it ever to be given to the public, for the identities would all be exposed ruthlessly. Besides, no one would believe it: it seems too improbable, being real life. It will be more improbable before we finish the adventure, I suspect. Can I trust your discretion to keep it secret? You know, I have a deal of skepticism about the best of women."

Helene reddened under that keen glance, and he saw that he had offended her.

"I beg your pardon: I know that we shall work it out together, with absolute mutual trust."

Such an earnest vibrance was in his voice that somehow she was reminded of another voice: her mind went back to the neglected letter to Jack. What could have caused her to be so remiss? She would not let herself dwell on the subject - instead, with a surprising deftness, she caught up Shirley's own cue, for a staggering question of her own.

"Are you sure that you have absolutely confided in me? Did you start at the beginning, when you told the story to-day."

"What do you mean?" and Shirley caught the glance sharply.

"Your unusual rapidity of action, Mr. Shirley, for a mere interested friend! It is queer how wonderfully your mind has connected this work, and the various accidental happenings, to evolve this clever ruse in which I am to assist. It doesn't seem so amateurish as you would make it. You seem mysterious to me."

"Do you think I am the voice? Here is a chance for real

detective work, if you can double the game, and capture me?" was the laughing retort. "I don't believe you trust me."

The girl stood up before him, and after one deep look, her eyes fell before his. Those exquisite lashes sent a tiny flutter through the case-hardened heart of the club man, despite his desperate determination to be a Stoic.

"I do trust you," the voice was impetuous, almost petulant. "You are a real man: I merely give you credit for being better than the class of rich young men of whom you pretend to be an absolute type. But there, I waste words and time. Is my costume for this little opera boufe satisfactory to you? Do you like my warpaint and battle armor?"

She stood before him, a glorious bird of paradise. The wanton display of a maddening curve of slender ankle, through the slash of the clinging gown imparted just the needed allurement to stamp her as a Vestal of the temple of Madness. The cunning simplicity of the draping over her shoulders - luminous with the iridescent gleam of ivory skin beneath, accentuated by the voluptuous beauty of her youthful bosom - the fleeting change of colors and contours as she slowly turned about in this maddening soul-trap of silk and laces - all these were not lost on the senses of Shirley. As the depths of those blue eyes opened before his gaze, a mad, a ridiculous aching to crush her in his arms, surprised the professional consulting criminologist! For this swift instant, all memory of the Van Cleft case, of every other problem, was driven from his mind, as a blinding blast of seething desire surged about him.

Then the old resolution, the conquering will of the man of one purpose, beat back the flames of this threatening conflagration. His eyes narrowed, his hands dropped to his side, and he squinted at her with the frigid dissective gaze of an artist studying the curves of a model.

"You must rouge your cheeks more, blue your eyelids and redden your lips even yet. Then be generous with the powder

- and that wonderful perfume."

An inscrutable smile played about the sensitive lips, as Helene turned to her dressing-table. Shirley stood with his face to the window; he did not observe it, nor would he have understood its menace to his own peace of mind. Helene, however, did. She was a woman.

"May I smoke a cigarette? I am afraid I am almost a fiend, for I seem to crave the foolish comfort that I imagine they give, in times of nervous drain."

"No, Lollypop's little Bonton Tootems enjoys their fragrance. Don't ever ask me again. I have completed the mural decoration with futurist extravagance in the color scheme. My cloak, sir!"

He tossed it about her, and took up his hat and gold-headed stick. With a final glance at his own careful make-up, he started after her for the street.

"Some chikabiddy!" was the remark of the clerk to the head bell-boy. The words reached the ears of Shirley and Helene. Her hand trembled on his arm as they entered a waiting taxicab. She looked pathetically at him, as she asked.

"Don't you think I am interested, sincere and loyal, to brave such remarks as these, and the other worse things they will say before long? I wouldn't dare do this, if I were not sure that no one in America but you and Mr. Holloway knows me. To wear this horrid stuff on my face - to dress in these vulgar clothes - to impersonate such a girl! You know I'm not nearly as bad as I'm painted!"

Shirley clasped her white-gloved hand and nodded. He was studying the pedestrians for a familiar twain of faces. He was not disappointed, as the car swung into Broadway.

"Look - those two men have been following me wherever I

have gone. They are a pair of old-fashioned pirates. Don't forget their faces!"

CHAPTER IX

IN THE GARDEN OF TEMPTATION

Their destination, one of the score of tango tea-rooms which had sprung to mushroom popularity within the year, was soon reached. Leaning heavily upon his stick, limping like his aged model, and spluttering impatiently, Shirley was assisted by the uniformed door man into the lobby. Helene followed meekly. Four hat boys from the check-room made the conventional scramble for his greatcoat, hat and stick, nearly upsetting him in their eagerness. Then Shirley led the way into the half light of the tropical, indoor garden, picking a way through the tables to a distant wall seat, embowered with electric grapes and artificial vines.

"Sit down, my darling child," said the pseudo Grimsby, as he dropped into a seat behind the table, which was protected from the lights, and furthest away from any possible visitors. "We are early, avoiding the crush. Soon the crowd will be here. We must have some champagne at once, to assist me in my defensive tactics. You will have to do most of the talking. Remember, we are going to the Winter Garden musical review when we leave here: you may tell this to whom you will."

Helene looked about curiously, as the big tea-room began to fill with its usual late afternoon crowd of patrons, - young, old and indeterminate in age. Women of maturely years, young misses from "finishing" schools, demimondaine, social "bounders" deluded by the glitter of their own jewelry and the thrill of their wasted money that they were climbing into New York society - these and other curious types rubbed elbows in this melting pot of folly. The tinkle of glasses, the increasing buzz of conversation, the empty laughter of too many emptied cocktail glasses mingled with the droning music of an Hawaiian string quartette in the far corner.

Suddenly, with banging tampani and the crash of cymbals, rattle of tambourines and beating of tomtoms, the barbaric Ethiopians of the dancing orchestra began their syncopated outrages against every known law of harmony - swinging weirdly into the bewitching, tickling, tingling rhythm of a maxixe.

"How strange!" murmured Helene, as the waiter brought them some champagne and indigestible pastries - the true ingredients of 'dansant the'.

"Yes, on with the dance-let joy be unrefined! The fall of the Roman Empire was the bounce of a rubber nursery ball, compared with this New York avalanche of luxurious satiation! Now, my child, old Da-da, is going to become too intoxicated to talk three words to any of these gallants and their lassies. Grimsby did not write a monologue for me, so I must pantomime: you will have to carry the speaking part of our playlet. Flatter them - but don't leave my side to dance!"

The first bottle of wine had been carried away by the waiter, (half emptied it is true,) as he filled a second order. Shirley shielded his face beneath a drooping spray of artificial blooms from the top of their wallbower. Several young men were approaching them, and the criminologist noted with relief that they evidenced their afternoon libations even so early. Eyes dulled with over-stimulus were the less analytical. Chance was favoring him. The newcomers were garbed in that debonair and "cultured" modishness so dear to the hearts of magazine illustrators. Faces, weak with sunken cheek lines, strong in creases of selfishness, darkened by the brush strokes of nocturnal excesses and seared, all of them with the brand mark of inbred rascality, identified them to Shirley as members of that shrewd class of sycophants who feast on the follies of the more amateurish moths of the Broadway Candles.

"Hello, old pop Grimsby!"

"You're in the dark of the moon, Grimmie! I couldn't make you out but for those horn rimmed head lights."

"Welcome to the joy-parlor, old scout."

The greetings of the juvenile buzzards varied only in phraseology: their portent was identical: "Open wine."

"Poor Mr Grimsby is so ill this afternoon, but sit down and have something with us," volunteered Helene tremulously.

The bees gathered about the table to feast on the vinous honey, while Shirley, mumbling a few words, maintained his partial obscurity, with one hand to his forehead.

"Fine boysh, m'deah. Boysh, meet little Bonbon - my protashsh!"

Little Bonbon was a pronounced attraction. Her vivacious charm drew the eyes away from Shirley, who studied the expressions of the weasel faces about him. The girl's heart sickened under the brutal frankness of a dozen calculating eyes, yet she valiantly maintained her part, while Shirley marveled at her clever simulation of silly, giggly, semi-intoxication. One youth deserted them to disappear through the distant dining room entrance. The comments about the table were interesting to the keen-eared masquerader.

"Old Grimsby's picked a live one, this time!" - "What show is she with?" - "Won't Pinkie be sore?" The criminologist was not left to wonder as to the identity of "Pinkie," for an older man, walking behind a red-headed girl in a luridly modern gown, approached the table with the absent guest. The men were talking earnestly, the girl staring angrily at Shirley's, beautiful companion.

"Hey, here come's Reggie! Sit down, Reg. Pop has passed away, but his credit is still strong."

"There's Pinkie - come, my dear, and join the Ladies' Aid Society and have a lemonade," jested another youth, making a place for the girl in the aisle.

Pinkie's dark-haired companion sank somewhat unsteadily into a chair next the girl. He frowned and rubbed his forehead, as though to clear his mind for needed concentration. He shook Shirley's arm, and spoke sharply.

"Look up; Grimmie. I never saw you feel your wine so early in the afternoon. It was a lucky day for me on Wall Street, so I celebrated myself. You are here earlier than usual. Everybody have some champagne with me."

As he beckoned to the waiter, the red-haired girl bestowed a murderous look upon Helene, who was sniffing some flowers which she had drawn from the vase on the table.

"Who's that Jane?" she demanded, her voice-shaking with jealousy. "Grimmie, you act as if you were doped. Introduce us to your swell friend. Wake him, Reg Warren."

Helene's jeweled white hand protected the safety-first dozing of her companion, as, through the interstices of his fingers, he studied the inscrutable difference between the face of Warren and the other youths about them.

"Let Pop dream of a new way to make a million!" laughed one young man. "His money grows while he sleeps."

"Yes, let him dream on," laughed Helene, with a shrill giggle. "When he makes that extra million he can star me on Broadway, in my own show. He, he!"

"You'll have to spend half of it at John the Barber's getting your voice marceled and your face manicured," snarled Pinkie. "Come, Reg, and dance with me: these bounders bore me."

"Run along, Pinkie, and fox-trot your grouch away with Shine Taylor. Here comes the wine I ordered - What's your name, girlie? Where did you meet Grimsby?"

"Oh, we're old friends," and Helene maliciously spilled a bottle over the interrogator's waistcoat, as she reached forward to shake his hand. "My name's Bonbon, you wouldn't believe me if I told you my real name, anyway. Who are you?"

"I'm not Neptune," he retorted, as he mopped the bubbles with a napkin. "You've started in badly." Shirley mentally disagreed. His stupor still obsessed him, but he noted with interest that Warren paid the check for his bottle with a new one-hundred dollar bill. Warren could elicit nothing from Helene but silly laughter, and so he arose impatiently, as Shine Taylor returned to whisper something in his ear. "I must be getting back to my apartment. Bring Grimsby up to it to-night: a little bromo will bring him back to the land of the living. I'll have a jolly crowd there - top floor of the Somerset, on Fifty-sixth Street, you know, near Sixth Avenue. Come up after the show."

"We're going to the Winter Garden," suggested Helene, at a nudge from Shirley, and Warren nodded.

"I'll try to see you later, anyway. Goodbye!"

Losing interest in the proceedings, as the time for reckoning the bill approached, the other gallants followed these two. Alone, again, Shirley ordered some black coffee, and smiled at his assistant.

"He told the truth for once."

"What do you mean?"

"He will try to see us later. That man is a member of the murderous clan whom we seek. 'To-night is the night' for the exit of William Grimsby - but, perhaps we may have a stage wait which will surprise them."

Gradually the guests thinned out in the tea-room, but Shirley cautiously waited until the last.

"Do you believe these young men are all members of the gang?" asked the girl. "Why do you suppose these men are all criminals? They surely look a bad lot."

"There are two general reasons why men go wrong. One is hard luck, aided by tempting opportunity - they hope to make a success out of failure, and then keep on the straight path for the rest of their lives. Such men are the absconders, the forgers, the bank-wreckers, and even the petty thieves. But once branded with the prison bars and stripes, they seldom find it possible to turn against the tide in which they find themselves: so they become habitual offenders. They are the easiest criminals to detect. The second class are the born crooks, who are lazy, sharp-witted and without enough will-power to battle against the problems of honesty in work. It is easy enough to succeed if a man is clever and unscrupulous without a shred of generosity. The hard problem is to be affectionate, human, and conquer every-day battles by remaining actively honest, when your rivals are not straight. The born crook is safer from prison than the weakling of the first class." He looked down at the coffee, and then continued.

"I do not believe all these young men are in this curious plot. They are merely the small fry of the fishing banks: they are petty rascals, with occasional big game. But somewhere, behind this sinister machine, is a guiding hand on the throttle, a brain which is profound, an eye which is all-seeing and a heart as cold as an Antartic mountain. There is the exceptional type of criminal who is greedy - for money and its luxurious possibilities; selfish - with regard for no other heart in the world; crafty - with the cunning of an Apache, enjoying the thrill of crime and cruelty; refined and vainglorious - with pride in his skill to thwart justice and confidence in his ability to continually broaden the scope of his work. Crime is the ruling passion of this unknown man. And the way to catch him is by using that passion as a bait upon the hook. I am the wriggling little angle worm who will dangle before his eyes to-night. But I do not expect to land him - I merely purpose to learn his identity, to draw the net of the law about him, in such a way as to keep the Grimsby and Van Cleft names from the case."

"And how can that be done?"

"That, young lady, is my 'fatal secret.' The subplot developing within my mind is still nebulous with me, - you would lose all interest, as would I, if you knew what was going to happen. But the time has passed, and now we can go to the theatre. I bought the tickets by messenger this afternoon. I will let you do the talking to the chauffeur and the usher."

They left the tea-room, the last guests out.

It was a touching sight to see the elderly gentleman supported on one side by a fat French waiter, and on the opposite, by the solicitous girl. The old Civil War wound was unusually troublesome.

CHAPTER X

WHEN IT'S DARK IN THE PARK

At the entrance of the restaurant the starter tooted his shrill whistle, and a driver began to crank his automobile in the waiting line of cars. According to the rules of the taxi stands he was next in order. But, as is frequently the custom in the hotly contested district of "good fares" another car "cut in" from across the street. This taxi swung quickly around and drew up before the waiting criminologist.

Grunting and mumbling, as though still deep in his cups, Monty allowed himself to be half pushed, half lifted into the car by the attendant. Helene followed him. "Winter Garden," she directed, and the machine sped away, while the thwarted driver in the rear sent a volley of anathemas after his successful competitor.

Shirley scrutinized the interior of the machine, but there seemed nothing to distinguish it from the thousands of other piratical craft which pillage the public with the aid of the taximeter clock on the port beam! Soon they were at the big Broadway playhouse, where Shirley floundered out first, after the ungallant manner of many sere-and-yellow beaux. He swayed unsteadily, teetering on his cane, as Helene leaped lightly to the sidewalk beside him. The driver stood by the door of the car, leering at him.

"Here, keep the change," and Shirley handed him a

generous bill.

"Shall I wait fer ye, gov'nor? I ain't got no call to-night. I'll be around here all evening."

The criminologist nodded, and the chauffeur handed Helene the carriage number check.

"Don't let 'em steal de old gink, inside, girlie. He's strong fer de chorus chickens."

Helene shuddered before the hawk-like glare of his malevolent eyes, but in her part, she shook her head with a laugh, and followed airily after her escort.

"Good-evening, sir. Back again to-night, I see," volunteered the ticket taker, to whom William Grimsby was a familiar visitant. Shirley reeled with steadied and studied equilibrium, into the foyer of the theatre, as he nodded. Their seats were purposely in the rear of a side box, well protected from the audience by the holders of the front positions. The criminologist appeared to relapse into dreams of bygone days, while his companion peered into the vast audience and then at the nimble limbed chorus on the stage with piquant curiosity.

"For years I wanted to see an American stage and an American audience," she confided in an undertone, "and to think that when I do so, it is acting myself, on the other side of the footlights in a stranger, more dramatic part than any one else in the theatre. A curious world, isn't it?"

Shirley breathed deeply, drinking in the maddening perfume of her glorious hair, so perilously near his own face. The shimmer of her shoulders, the adorable curves of that enticing scarlet mouth murmuring so near his own, and yet so far away, in this soul-racking game of make-believe, stirred his blood as nothing else had done in all the kalaediscopic years.

"Yes, a more than curious world. How things have changed

since last evening when I planned a sleepy evening at the opera. I wonder what the outcome will be?"

Helene looked up at him quickly, then as suddenly toward the Russian danseuse within the golden frame of the great proscenium. The orchestra, with its maddening Slavic music, stirred her pulses with a strange telepathy. The evening wore along, until the final curtain. Shirley, with cumbersome effort helped her with her cloak, dropping his hat and stick more than once in simulated awkwardness. The electric numerals of the carriage call soon brought the grimy-faced chauffeur.

"Jack on the spot, gov'nor, that's me!" and he swung the door open.

"We'll go get some supper - no, we'll take little 'scursion in Central Park, first," and his voice was thick, "correct, cabbie. Drive us shru Central Park."

"Are you going to take a chance in a dark park?" Helene asked him, as they sat within the car, while the chauffeur cranked. Shirley was sharply observing the man. A pedestrian crossed directly in front of the machine, brushing against the driver, as he fumbled with the lamp. If there were an interchange of words, the criminologist could not detect it.

"Surely. The park is good. We can be free of interference from the police. Are you afraid?"

"No - " yet, it was a pardonably weak little voice which uttered the valiant monosyllable.

"Here, Miss Marigold. Take this revolver. Don't use it until you have to, but then don't hesitate a second."

The machine started slowly up the street. Shirley groped about the sides and bottom of the car, to make sure that no one could be concealed within it. They were advancing up Broadway in leisurely fashion. It might have been for the purpose of allowing some to follow. Shirley wondered, then sniffed the air suspiciously. The girl looked at him with a silent question.

"Quick, tear off your glove and let me have that diamond ring I noticed on your finger, the large solitaire, not the dinner ring."

Unquestioningly she obeyed. There was a strange Oriental odor in the car - suggestive of an incense. The car was gliding up Central Park West, toward one of the road entrances into the Park proper. Shirley's hand clutched the ring, tensely. The driver, tactfully looking straight to the front, gave no heed to the occupants of the Death Car. He was, by this time speeding too rapidly for either of his passengers to have leaped out without injury. Shirley understood the smoothness of the voice's system, by now. His hand slid to the top of the glass door pane, on the right. Down the glass, across the bottom, down from the other corner, and then over the top line, he cut with the diamond, using a peculiar pressure. He rose to his feet, gave the lower part of the pane a sharp tap. The glass, practically cut loose from its case, now dropped and would have slid out to the roadway with a crash had he not dexterously caught it, to draw it into the car. Quickly he repeated the operation with the door pane at the left. A nauseating, weakening something in the car sent Helene's head spinning; she choked for breath and lay back weakly, despite her will. Shirley turned to the small glass square in the rear. This came out more easily. He lay the glass with the others, on the floor of the car. The good clear air whirled through the openings, reviving the girl.

"Keep your eyes open, and that revolver ready. Now is the time. Pretend to sleep."

Shirley had drawn his own automatic by this time, and he realized that the machine was slowing down. The chauffeur, as they passed a walk light, looked back, observing that the two were apparently unconscious. He slowed down still more, and tooted his horn three times. A large touring car passed them, to stop some distance ahead. Then it sped on, as Shirley's taxi followed lazily.

A figure suddenly came out of the darkness of the road. The driver stopped the taxi, and walked around the front, as though to adjust the lamp. The door opened slowly. A face covered with a black handkerchief obtruded. A hand slid up the detective's knee, along his side toward the abdomen, and a protruding thumb began a singular pressure directly below the criminologist's heart. Shirley's analysis for Dr. MacDonald had been correct! But jiu-jitsu is essentially a game for two.

Shirley's left hand suddenly shot forth to the neck of his assailant. His muscular fingers closed in a deft and vice-like pinch directly below the silk handkerchief. It was the pneumogastric nerve, which he reached: a nerve which, when deadened by Oriental skill, paralyzes the vocal chords. Not a sound emanated from the mysterious man, even when Shirley's right hand shot forward, under the chin of the other, for a deft blow across the thorax. The other tumbled backward.

"What's wrong, Chief? Too much gas?" cried the chauffeur rushing to the side of the fallen man. As the driver dropped to his knees, Shirley flung himself like a tiger upon the rascal's back. The struggle was brief - the same silent silencer accomplished its purpose. Before the man knew what had happened to him, he was dragged inside the car, and another deft pinch sent him to oblivion!

"Hit him over the forehead with the butt of the revolver if he opens his mouth," grunted Shirley. "This is the chauffeur, now I'll get the other one."

Just then a cry came from the darkness: it was a passing patrolman.

"What you doing in that auto?"

But Shirley waited for no parley-explanations, showing his hand, laying the whole scandal before the morning edition of the newspapers, were all out of question now. He must take up the pursuit later. He caught up, the chauffeur's cap, sprang into the driver's seat, and the car shot forward like a race horse as he threw forward the lever. The astonished policeman was within twenty-five yards of the spot, when the auto disappeared in the darkness. He pursued it vainly.

A few moments later, a man with a handkerchief across his face, groaned and then raised himself on his elbow, there in the roadway. He could not remember where he was, nor why. Slowly he crawled on hands and knees, into the rhododendrons by the roadside, where he again lost consciousness.

A big touring car rounded the curve of the roadway.

"Not a sign of the Chief," said the driver. "He must have gone back to the garage with the Monk. But that's a fool idea. Let's get down there right away."

The injured man's memory returned, and he rose stiffly to his feet. He limped out of the Park, putting away the handkerchief, muttering profanity and trying to fathom the mystery. As nearly as he could reason it out, he must have been struck by another machine from the rear.

Far up in the northernmost driveway of the Park, where shrub grown banks and rocky uplands shelter the thoroughfares, Shirley stopped his runaway taxicab.

"Let me have his rubber coat, for I'm going to hide this car out on Long Island. It's a long ride, but this man and his machine will disappear as completely as though they had been dumped in the ocean."

Shirley manacled the prisoner, and gagged him with a tightly knotted handkerchief. He put the greatcoat of Grimsby's about Helene's shoulders, as he brought her to the front seat of the machine. Then he shut the doors on the prisoner, and drove the automobile out through the Easterly entrance of the park.

"I'm not really brave, Mr. Montague," said the tired voice at his side. "I'm so glad I'm sitting by you, instead of back inside. We will be home soon, won't we? I'm so exhausted - my first day in a strange country, you know."

Shirley, with the skill of a racing expert, guided the machine through the maze of streets toward the Bridge over the East River. The touch of that sweet shoulder, as it unconsciously nestled against his own, sent through him a tremor which he had not experienced during the weird silent battle in the dark.

"A strange night, in a strange country. Are you sorry you tried it?"

With a sidelong glance, he caught the starry light in her eyes as she looked up at him: there seemed more than the mere reflection of passing street lamps.

"A wonderful night: I'm glad, so glad, not sorry," was her dreamy response. She lapsed into silence as the somnolent drone of the motor and the whirr of the wheels caused the tired eyes to close sleepily.

When he looked at her again, as they were speeding down the bridge Plaza in Long Island City, she was dozing. The drowsy head touched his shoulder; she seemed like a child, worn out with games, trustingly asleep in the care of a big, strong brother.

CHAPTER XI

A TURN IN THE TRAIL

Helene was still asleep when Shirley stopped the engine of the taxi before a stately Colonial mansion seated back among the pines of a beautiful Long Island estate. They had been driving for more than an hour. The girl stirred languorously as he strove to awaken her. She murmured drowsily:

"No, Jack, dear. Emphatically no. Let's not talk about it any more, dear boy."

"Who can Jack be?" and a surprising pang shot through Montague Shirley's heart. "Jack, dear! Well, and what's it my business. She is a stranger. She lives her life and I mine. But, at any rate, that settles some silly things I've been thinking. I'm less awake than she is."

This time he tried with better success, and Helene rubbed her eyes, with hands stiffened by the brisk bite of the chill wind. She gazed at the dimly lit house, at the big figure beside her, as Shirley sprang to the ground - then remembered it all, and trembled despite herself.

"Oh, it's you, Mr. Shirley," and she summoned up a little throaty laugh, as she arose stiffly. "What a queer place to be in!"

"We are a long way from New York's white lights, Miss

Marigold. This is the country home of a good old friend of mine. You can remain here for the rest of the night, as his wife's guest. To-morrow, when you are rested, he can send you to the city in one of his cars."

"You are the most curious man in two continents. I am bewildered. First, you kidnap a chauffeur and privateer his car, then me. Now you besiege a friend and wish to leave me on his doorstep as a foundling."

"I'm sorry - it's the exigency of war! We must finish what we started. This is the only place I know where I could thoroughly hide my trail. We must wake up Jim, but first I will have a look at our guest."

Shirley walked around the car, shooting the beam from his pocket flashlight in through the open window of the taxi, to be met by the wicked black eyes of his prisoner, who uttered volumes of unpronounceable hatred.

"You are still with us, little bright eyes. A pleasant trip, I trust? I hope you found the air good - I tried to improve the ventilation for your benefit, as well as my own." Only a subdued gurgle answered him.

"Oh, what will they think of me - in this immodest gown, with this paint on my face, and at this hour of night?" pleaded Helene, as he started toward the door of the mansion.

"It would be awful at that," and Shirley paused at the beseeching tone of the girl. "I want you to meet Mrs. Jim as well as Jim. I am afraid they would think this was the echo of an old college escapade, and misjudge you. Let me think - "

He led her to a little summer-house close by, and tucked the big coat about her as he added: "It's dark here - the wind doesn't reach you, and I'll take you back to town in five minutes. Will that do?"

As she nodded, he hurried to the door where he yanked vigorously at the bell. An angry head protruded from an upper story, after many encores of the peals.

"Aw, what the dickens? Go some place else and find out!"

"Jim, Jim. It's Monty! Come down and let me in quick."

The window closed with a bang as the head was withdrawn, while a light soon appeared in the beveled panes of the big front door.

"You poor boob," was the cheerful greeting as it swung wide, "What brings you out here? I thought it was the usual joy party which had lost its way. They always pick me out for an information bureau. Come on in!"

Shirley spoke rapidly, in a low tone. The girl in the dark summer-house marveled at the rapid change of mien, as Jim suddenly ran down the steps to gaze into the taxicab, then nodding to Shirley. The house-holder as promptly returned through his front door, while Shirley swiftly unmanacled the prisoner enough to let him walk, stiff and awkward from the long ordeal in the car. The stern grip, of his captor prompted obedience.

Friend Jim had appeared with warmer garments, carrying a lantern. At the door of the stable Jim's stentorian yell to the groom seemed useless, but the two men entered. Helene felt miserably weak and deserted, in the chill night, but she was cheered by seeing the energetic Shirley reappear, pushing open the doors of the garage, which was connected with the stable. He hurried to the deserted taxicab, where he seemed busied for several minutes, the glow of his pocket lamp shooting out now and then. Through the door of the garage a long, rakish-looking racing car was being pushed out by Jim and his sleepy groom. There was a cheery shout from the taxi, and Helene heard a ripping sound. Shirley reappeared, carrying an oblong box.

"I have the gas generator: - it was built in, under the seat, and controlled by a battery wire from the front lamp, Jim. A nice little mechanism. Well, old pal, please apologize to Mrs. Merrivale for my rude interruption of her beauty sleep. Keep a fatherly eye on Gentleman Mike, and the taxicab under cover. I'll communicate with you very soon. So long."

To Helene's amazement, Shirley cranked the racer, jumped in and seemed to be starting away without her, down the sweep of the driveway. Could he have forgotten her? The man must indeed be mad, as some of his actions indicated! But her aroused indignation was turned to admiration of his finesse, for suddenly he veered the lights of the car toward the garage door, throwing them in the faces of Jim and his servant. He leaped out again, walking past the place of concealment.

"Slip into the car, while I go inside with them. I'll come out on the run, and no one will be the wiser."

With this passing stage direction he rushed toward his accomodating friend, with some final directions. They were apparently humorous in content, for both the other men roared with mirth, as he walked inside the building, with them, an arm around the shoulder of each. Helene obeyed him, hiding as best she could in the low seat of the throbbing machine. As Shirley returned, Jim Merrivale was still laughing blithely.

"Good-bye, you old maniac: you'll be the death of me. I'll take care of the star boarder, however, and feed him champagne and mushrooms."

With a roar, Shirley started the engines, as he bounced into the seat, and they sped down the curving driveway, with Helene leaning forward, unobserved.

"There, we've had a little by-play that friend Jim didn't guess. I always enjoy a little intrigue," he laughed, as they whizzed along toward distant New York. "But, I had to lie, and lie, and lie - like the light that lies in women's eyes. What a jolly game!"

He was a big boy, happy in the excitement, and bubbling with his superabundance of vitality. Helene felt curiously drawn toward him, in this mood: she remembered a little paragraph she had read in a book that day:

"A woman loves a man for the boy spirit that she discovers in him: she loves him out of pity when it dies!" Then she fearsomely changed the current of her thoughts, to complain pathetically of the cold wind!

"There, now, I am so thoughtless," was his apology, as he stopped the car, to wrap the overcoat more closely about her, and tuck her comfortably in a big fur. Through the darkened streets of the suburb they raced, entering the silent factory districts, which presaged the nearness of the river. It was well on toward daybreak before they rolled over the Queensboro Bridge to Manhattan. It was his second day without sleep, but Shirley was sustained by the bizarre nature of the exploit: he could have kept at the steering wheel for an eternity.

"Are you glad we're getting back?" he asked. Helene shook her head, then she answered dreamily.

"Do you remember something from one of Browning's poems, that I do? It's just silly for us, but I understand it better now."

Shirley surprised her by quoting it, as he looked ahead into the dark street through which they swung, his unswerving hand steady on the wheel:

> "What if we still ride on, we two,
> With life forever old yet new,
> Changed not in kind, but in degree,
> The instant made eternity, -
> And heaven just prove that I and she
> Ride, ride together, forever ride?"

Eustace Hale Ball

A quick flush, not caused by the biting wind, suffused her cheek beneath the remnants of the rouge. Then she laughed up at him appreciatively.

"Curious how our minds ran that way, and hit the very same poem, wasn't it?"

Shirley smiled back, as he swung down Fifth Avenue.

"Not so curious after all!"

Soon they drew up before the ornate portal of the California Hotel, where late arrivals were so customary as to cause no comment. He bade her good-night, words seeming futile after their long hours together. The drive in the car to the club was short. Paddy the door man was instructed to send down to Shirley's own garage for a mechanic to store the car until further orders. The criminologist had ere this rubbed off his grease paint, so that his appearance was not unusual. Once in his rooms he treated himself to a piping hot shower, cleaned off the powder from his dark locks, and as he smoked a soothing cigarette, in his bathrobe, studied the mechanism of the gas generator for a few moments.

"That was made by an expert who understands infernal machines with a malevolent genius. I must look out for him," he mused. "Well, I promised Professor MacDonald that I would not sleep until I had come face to face with the voice. I have fulfilled the vow: now for forgetfulness."

He tumbled into bed, but not to oblivion. For his dreams were disturbed by tantalizing visions of certain sun-gold locks and blue eyes not at all in their simple connection with the business end of the Van Cleft mystery.

CHAPTER XII

THE HAND OF THE VOICE

It took stoicism to the Nth degree for Shirley to respond to the early telephone call next morning, from the clerk of the club. A few minutes of violent exercise, in the hand ball court, the plunge, a short swim in the natatorium and a rub down from the Swedish masseur, however, brought him around to the mood for another adventure. Sending for the racing car he began the round-up of details. There was, first of all, Captain Cronin to be visited in Bellevue. Here he was agreeably surprised to find the detective chief recuperating with the abettance of his rugged Celtic physique. The nurse told Shirley that another day's treatment would allow the Captain to return to his own home: Shirley knew this meant the executive office of the Holland Detective Agency.

"And sure, Monty, when I have a free foot once again, I'm going to apply it to them gangsters who put me to sleep."

"Just what I want you to do, Captain! I 'phoned to your men this morning while I had breakfast at the club: they have that taxicab which was left near Van Cleft's house. It's put away safely, Cleary said. There are two gangsters where the dogs won't bite them; today they are sending out to Jim Merrivale's house to get the third and he'll be busy with a little private third degree. I have no evidence which would connect the man who tried to kill me last night with the other murders, except in a circumstantial way. What I must do is to follow up the

Eustace Hale Ball

trail, and get the gentleman carrying out the bales, in other words, with the goods on him."

"You'll get him, Monty, if I know you. The fellow hasn't called up at all on the telephone to-day. I think he's afraid of you."

"No, Captain Cronin, not that! He's up to some new game. Well, I'm off - take care of yourself and don't eat anything the nurse doesn't bring you with her own hands. I wouldn't put anything past this gang."

He shook hands and hurried out of the hospital, with several more errands to complete. He looked vainly about him for the gray racing-car. It was gone! Here was another unexpected interference with his work, and Shirley, sotto voce, expressed himself more practically than politely. He hurried to an ambulance driver who stood in a doorway, solacing his jangled nerves with a corn-cob smoke.

"Neighbor, did you see any one take the gray car standing here a few minutes ago?"

"Yep, a feller just came out of the hospital entry, cranked her and jumped in."

"How long ago?"

"Well, I just returned with a suicide actor case five minutes ago."

"Then you might have seen him enter first?"

"Nope. Not a sign. All I seen was the way he cranked the machine, and he didn't waste any elbow grease doin' it, either. He knew the trick. That's what I thought when I seen him, even if he did look like a dude."

Shirley hurried to the entry once more. This was the only

portal through which visitors were admitted to the hospital for the purpose of calling on patients. He hastened to the uniformed attendant who took down the names of all applicants. This man, upon inquiry, was a trifle dubious. True, there had been two Italian women and before them - yes, there had been a young chap with a green velour hat, and white spats. He had asked about a Captain Cronin, and when told that a visitor was already seeing the patient, agreed to wait outside. It had been about five minutes before. The man was indefinite about more details. Shirley hurried to the telephone booth in the corridor. To Headquarters he reported the theft of car "99835 N.Y.," giving a description of its special features and its make. This warning he knew would be telephoned to all stations within five minutes, so that every policeman in New York would be on the lookout for the missing machine. Satisfied, he left the hospital, to walk across the long block to the nearest north and south avenue, where he might catch a surface car.

Suddenly he halted, to mutter in astonishment at a sight which was the surprise of the morning: it was the missing car standing peacefully on the next corner.

"I wonder what that means?" he murmured, as he stopped to study with great interest the window of an Italian green grocer. A sidelong glance at the car and its surroundings revealed nothing out of the way. He retraced his steps to the hospital, wasted ten minutes with a cigarette or two, and still no one seemed to take an interest in the automobile. Finally he walked up to the car, trying the lock of which he had the only key. Apparently it had been untampered with, for the key worked perfectly. Here was Jim Merrivale's car, a good three hundred yards away from the place where he had locked it to prevent any moving. He felt certain that keen eyes had him under surveillance, yet he could not observe any observers within the range of his own vision. It was simply a stupid, quiet slum neighborhood and at the time, unusually deserted by the customary hordes of children and dogs!

What had been the purpose in moving it such a short distance?

Where had it been in the twenty-five minutes since he had left it at the entrance to the hospital?

Why had it been left here, of all places, where he would naturally walk if desirous of taking a street-car?

There seemed no immediate answer to the conundrums. So, he nonchalantly clambered into the car, after cranking it. The mechanism seemed in perfect order. Puzzled, he started to speed up the street, when he observed a white envelope close by his foot, on the floor of the car.

He picked it up, and tearing it open quickly read this simple message.

"To whom it may concern: It is frequently advisable to mind your own business - is it not? Answer: Yes!"

"Huh," grunted Shirley. "While not thrilling in originality, it is a lasting truth which nobody can deny. I'll save this and frame it on the walls of my rooms."

As he drove around the corner and up the Avenue, there was suddenly a terrific explosion, which threw him completely out of the machine! The car, without a driver, its engines whirring madly, dashed into a helpless corner fruit stand, scattering oranges, bananas, apples and desolation in its wake, as it vainly endeavored to climb to the second story with super-mechanical intelligence! Shirley, stunned and bruised, fell to the pavement where he lay until an excited patrolman rushed to his rescue.

A little "first aid" work brought Shirley back to consciousness, and he stiffly rose to his feet, with a head throbbing too much for any real thinking.

"What's the matter with your auto?" cried the policeman. "Can't you run it? Let's see the number." The officer took out his notebook, to jot down the details according to police rules. Then he turned on Shirley in amazement. "Be gorry, it's car 99835 N.Y. I just wrote the number down when I came on post with my squad! This car is stolen. You come with me!"

Shirley had been adjusting the mechanism, and the wheels had ceased their whirring. He tried to expostulate in a dazed way, realizing that for once the department was working with a vengeful promptness. He was hoist by his own petard!

"I'm the owner of the car," he began, rubbing his aching forehead.

"What's yer name?"

"Montague Shirley!" The policeman laughed, as he caught the criminologist by the shoulder, and blew his whistle for another man from post duty.

"You lie. This car is owned by James Merrivale. You can't put over raw stuff like that on me. I'm no rookie - Here, Joe," (as the other policeman ran up through the growing, jeering crowd,) "watch this machine. This guy's one of them auto Raffles, and I done a good job when I lands him. I'm going to the station-house now."

The other policeman was examining the car, when he called to his fellow officer: "Here, Sim, did you see this car was blown up inside the seat?"

Shirley, his acuteness returned by this time, ran to the car eluding his captor's hold. He had not observed before the jagged shattered hole torn in the side of the leather side. It had all happened so swiftly, that his professional instincts were slow in reasserting themselves after the "buck" of the car.

"You're right," he exclaimed. "There's an alarm clock and a dry battery - the same man made this who built the gas-generator - "

"Whadd'ye mean - ain't you the feller after all?" asked the first patrolman, beginning to get dubious about his arrest.

"No, I am no thief. But just take me to the station-house quick, and turn in your report. Let this other man guard that car. Hurry up!"

"Say, feller, who do you think is making this arrest? You'll go to the station-house when I get ready."

"Then you're ready now," snapped the criminologist. "You'll see me discharged very promptly, when I speak to the Commissioner over the wire."

The officer was supercilious until the station-house was reached. He had heard this blatant talk before. What was his surprise when Shirley telephoned to the head of the Department and then called the Captain to the instrument.

"Release Mr. Shirley at once," was the crisp order. "Give him any men or assistance he needs."

"Well, whadd'ye know about that? Not even entered on the blotter to credit me with a good arrest!" The patrolman turned away in disgust.

"Do you want any of the reserves, sir?" The Captain was scrupulously polite.

"Not one. I'm going to study that machine again. You might detail a plain clothes man to walk along the other side of the street for luck. Good-day."

The automobile to which he returned was still the object of community interest. Shirley took the remains of the bomb which had caused his sudden elevation. The policeman approached him from the fruit store.

"The man wants damages for the stock you destroyed, mister.

I'll fix it up with him if you want - about twenty-five dollars will do."

"Well, hand him this five-dollar bill and see if that won't dry some of the imported tears," retorted Shirley with a laugh. In a few minutes he was bowling along on a surface car, to the club. There was no longer any use in trying to hide his identity or address, for the conspirators knew at least of his interest and assistance in the case: although in this as all others he was not known to be a professional sleuth.

In the quiet of his room he drew out magnifying glasses and other instruments for a thorough analysis of the remains of the infernal machine. He compared this with the mechanism of the gas-generator which had been placed in the seat of the Death taxi. There was evidence that it had come from the same source. Shirley sniffed at the generator and the peculiar odor still clinging to it was familiar.

"Well, I think I will have a little surprise for Mr. Voice, the next time we grapple, which will be an encore of his own tune, with a new verse!"

He went to a cabinet, took out a small glass vial, filled with a limpid liquid and placed it within his own pocket. Then he prepared for a new line of activities for the day. His first duty was a call on Pat Cleary, superintendent of the Holland Agency.

"The Captain is progressing splendidly," was his answer to the anxious query. "He will be back in the harness again to-morrow. How are the prisoners?"

"They have tried to break out twice and gave my doorman a black eye. But they got four in return: Nick is no mollycoddle, you know. I can't quite get the number of these fellows, for they are not registered down at Headquarters, in the Rogue's Gallery. Their finger-prints are new ones in this district, too. They look like imported birds, Mr. Shirley. What do you think?"

Cleary's opinion of the club man had been gaining in ascendency.

"They may be visitors from another city, but I think the state will keep them here as guests for a nice long time, Cleary. They say New York is inhospitable to strangers, but we occasionally pay for board and room from the funds of the taxpayers without a kick. We saved the day for the Van Clefts, all right. The paper told of a beautiful but quiet funeral ceremony, while the daughter has postponed her marriage for six months."

Then he recounted the adventure of the exploding car. Cleary lit his malodorous pipe, and shook his head thoughtfully.

"Young man, you know your own affairs best. But with all your money, you'd better take to the tall pines yourself, like these old guys in the 'Lobster Club.' That's the advice of a man who's in the business for money not glory. This is a bum game. They'll get me some day, some of these yeggs or bunk artists that I've sent away for recuperation, as the doctors call it. But I'm doing it for bread and beefsteak, while it lasts. You run along and play - a good way from the fire, or you'll get more than your fingers burnt. Take their hint and beat it while the beating's good."

A glint of steel shone from the eyes of the criminologist as he lit another cigarette and took up his walking-stick.

"Why, Cleary, this is what I call real sport. Why go hunting polar bears and tigers when we've got all this human game around the Gold Coast of Manhattan? I'm tired of furs: I want a few scalps. Good-morning."

As Cleary went up the stairway to renew the ginger of the Third Degree for the two prisoners, he smiled to himself, and muttered:

"The guy ain't such a boob as he looks: he's just a high-class nut. I'd enjoy it myself if it wasn't my regular work."

At Dick Holloway's office Shirley was greeted with an eager demand for his report of the former evening's activities. An envious look was on the face of the theatrical manager.

"Shucks, Monty! It's a shame that all this sport is private stock, and can't be bottled up and peddled to the public, for they're just crazy about gangster melodrama. They're paying opera prices for the old time ten-twent-and-thirt-melodrama, right on Broadway. Hurry up and get the man and I'll have him dramatized while the craze is rampant."

"Not while I own the copyright," retorted Shirley, "this is one of the chapters of my life that isn't going to be typewritten, much less the subject of gate-receipts."

"I'm not so certain of that," and Holloway's smile was quizzical.

"What do you mean? Who is this Helene Marigold? I have a right to know in a case like this."

"Good intuition, as far as you go. But you're guessing wrong, for she has nothing to do with my little joke. But why worry about her?" laughed Holloway. His friend had leaned forward, intensely, clutching his cane, with an unusually serious look on his face. Holloway had never seen Shirley take such an interest in any woman before. He arose from his desk-chair and walked to the broad window, which overlooked the thronging sidewalks of Broadway.

"Down there is the biggest, busiest street in the world filled with women of all hues and shades. This is the first time you ever looked so anxious about any combination of lace, curls, silks and gew-gaws before. You have been the bright and shining example of indifferent bachelor freedom which has made me - thrice divorced - so envious of your unalloyed, unalimonied joy. Don't betray the feet of clay which have supported my idol!"

The baffling smile of the debonair club man returned to Shirley's face, as he twitted back: "Purely an altruistic inquiry, Dick. I feared that you might be risking your own heart and the modicum of freedom which you still possess. But I'll wager a supper-party for four that I'll find out who she is, without either you or she telling me."

"Taken. At last I'm to have a free banquet, after years of business entertaining. You have met a girl who will match your wits - I expect the sparks to fly. Well, she's worth while - I might do worse - but in perfect fairness she ought to do better. How about it?"

"Yes, with Jack," and Shirley tapped the walking stick on the floor with an emphatic thump, while Holloway regarded him in startled surprise.

"Who is Jack?"

"You see - I am learning already. But, you and I are drifting from my task. I wish that you would take me to call on Miss Marigold, in my present lack of disguise. I do not care for that ancient garb any longer. It was stretching the chances rather far, but thanks to the darkness, the champagne, and good fortune, I succeeded in impersonating our aged friend without detection. I will not return to Grimsby's house, but propose now to get down to brass tacks with Mr. Voice, even though the tacks be hard to sit upon. I wish to use her as a bait, by taking her out to tea and getting a first-hand speaking acquaintance with these convivial assassins."

"Monty, you are wasting your talents outside the pages of a play manuscript, but we will make that call instanter."

In leisure, they promenaded up the crowded Gay Wide Way, through the noontime crowd of theatrical folk who dot the thoroughfare in this part of the city. His adversaries were to have every opportunity to observe his movements and draw their own conclusions. At the Hotel California new comment buzzed between the garrulous clerk and the switchboard person, at sight of the well-known manager and his prosperous-looking companion.

"Who is that come on?" asked the clerk of the bellboy.

"Sure, dat's Montague Shirley, one of dem rich ginks from de College Club on Forty-fourth Street, where I used to woik in de check room. If I had dat guy's money I'd buy a hotel like dis."

"Then I see where Holloway, with that blonde dame upstairs, will be putting on a new musical show, with a new angel. It's a great business, Miss Gwendolyn - no wonder they call it art." And the clerk removed a silk handkerchief from his coat cuff, to dust the register wistfully. "Why didn't I devote my talents to the drama instead of room-keys and due-bills?"

But Miss Gwendolyn was too busy talking to the Milwaukee drummer in Room 72 to formulate a logical reason. Shirley and Holloway improved the time by taking the elevator to the top floor where Helene greeted them at the door of her pretty apartment. She welcomed them happily, declaring it had been a lonesome morning.

"Weren't you resting from that long thrill of last night, in which you starred?" asked Holloway.

"It was too thrilling for me to sleep: I know I look a perfect frump, this morning. I tossed on the pillow, watching the dawn over your towering New York roofs, so nervous and almost miserable. But, with company, it's all right again."

Holloway laughed inwardly at the warmth of the glance which she bestowed upon Shirley. From the angle of an audience, he was beginning to observe a phase of this double play of personalities which was unseen by either of the participants. Two sleepless nights, after such a first evening together, and what then? He imagined the denouement, with a growing enjoyment of his vantage-point as the game advanced.

"To-day, I am reversing the usual progress of history," said Shirley, as he sat down in the window-seat. "From second juvenility I am returning to the first. In other words, I wish to become your adoring suitor in the role of Montague Shirley."

"I don't understand," and her eyes widened in wonder, not without an accompanying blush which did not escape Holloway.

"No longer a lamb in sheep's clothing, I want to entertain you, without the halo of William Grimsby's millions. I want to take tea with these gentle-voiced cut-throats, who after my warning to-day, are directing their attention to me." He narrated the narrow escape from death in the racing-car. Helene's eyes darkened with an uncertainty which he had hardly expected. Perhaps she would refuse to carry out their compact along these dangerous lines.

"Do you feel it wise to place yourself beneath this new menace?"

"The sword of Damocles is over me now, I know. To run would be a confession of weakness and open the field for his further activities, with the rear-guard continuously exposed. There is nothing like the personal equation. I will call at five this afternoon, if you are willing, Miss Marigold?"

"I will fight it out to the end," and she placed her warm hand firmly within his own. The two friends departed, Shirley retracing his steps to the club where many things were to be studied and planned. His system of debit and credit records of facts known and needed, was one which brought finite results. As he smoked and pondered at his ease, a tapping on the study door aroused him from his vagrant speculations. At his call, a respectful Japanese servant presented a note, just left by a messenger-boy. He tore the envelope and read it.

"Montague Shirley: - The third time is finis. As a friend you accomplished the purpose you sought. There is no grudge against you. Why seek one? It is fatal for you to remain in the city. Leave while you have time."

That was all. The chirography was the same as that upon the note of the racing-car episode. Shirley locked up the missive in his cabinet, and smiled at the increasing tenseness of the situation.

"The writer of these two notes may have an opportunity to leave town himself before long, to rest his nerves in the quiet valley of the Hudson, at Ossining. My friend the enemy will soon be realizing a deficit in his rolling-stock and gentlemanly assistants. Two automobiles and three prisoners to date. There should be additional results before midnight. I wonder where he gardens into fruition these flowers of crime?"

And even as he pondered, a curious scene was being enacted within a dozen city blocks of the commodious club house.

CHAPTER XIII

THE SPIDER'S WEB

The setting was a bleak and musty cellar, beneath an old stable of dingy, brick construction. The building had been modernized to the extent of one single decoration on the street front, an electric sign: "Garage." On the floor, level with the sidewalk, stood half a dozen automobiles of varied manufacture and age. Near the wide swinging doors of oak, stood a big, black limousine. Two taxicabs of the usual appearance occupied the space next to this, while a handsome machine faced them on the opposite side of the room. Two ancient machines were backed against the wall, in the rear.

In the basement beneath, several men were grouped in the front compartment, which was separated by a thick wooden partition from the rear of the cellar. Three dusty incandescents illuminated this space. In the back a curious arrangement of two large automobile headlights set on deal tables directed glaring rays toward the one door of the partition. In the center of the rear room was another table, standing behind a screen of wire gauze, at the bottom of which was cut a small semicircle, large enough for the protrusion of a white, tense hand, whose fingers were even now spasmodically clenching in nervous indication of fury. Behind either lamp was a heavy black screen, which effectually shut off ingress to that portion of the room.

The man standing between the table and the closed door of the partition, full in the light of the lamps, watched the hand as though fascinated. He could see nothing else, for behind the gauze all was darkness. Absolutely invisible, sat the possessor of the hand, observing the face of his interviewer, on the brighter side of the gauze.

"So, there's no word from the Monk?"

"No, chief. De bloke's disappeared. Either he got so much swag offen dis old Grimsby guy, after youse got de bumps, or he had cold feet and beat it wid de machine,"

"It's a crooked game on me." rasped the voice behind the screen. "I'll send him up for this. You know how far my lines go out. What about Dutch Jake and Ben the Bite?"

The man before the screen shook his head in helpless bewilderment There was a suggestion of fright in his manner, as well.

"Can't find out a t'ing, gov'nor. I hopes you don't blame me for dis. I'm doin' my share. Dey just disappears dat night w'en you sends 'em to shadder Van Cleft's joint. My calcerlation is - "

"I'm not paying you to calculate. I've trusted you and lost six thousand dollars' worth of automobiles for my pains. You can just calculate this, that unless I get some news about Jake, Ben and the Monk by this time tomorrow, I'll send some news down to Police headquarters on Lafayette Street that will make you wish you had never been born."

For some reason not difficult to guess, the suggestion had a galvanic effect on the bewildered one. His hands trembled as he raised them imploringly to the screen.

"Oh, gov'nor, wot have I done? Ain't I been on de level wid yez? Say, I ain't never even seen yez for de fourteen months I've been yer gobetween. I've been beat up by de cops, pinched and sent to de workhouse 'cause I wouldn't squeal, and now ye t'reatens me. Did I ever fall down on a trick ontil dis week? You'se ain't goin' ter welch on me, are you'se? I ain't no welcher meself, an' ye knows it."

The other snapped out curtly: "Very well, cut out the sob stuff. It's up to you to prove that there hasn't been a leak somewhere or a double cross. Send in those rummies, - I want to give them the once over again. There's a nigger in the woodpile somewhere, and I'm no abolitionist! Quick now. Get a wiggle on."

The hand was withdrawn from the little opening, as the lieutenant advanced into the front compartment of the cellar. He beckoned meaningly to the others to follow him. They obeyed with a slinking walk, which showed that they were obsessed by some great dread, in that unseen presence, in the heart of the spider-web!

"Which one of you is the stool pigeon," came the harsh query.

"W'y, gov'nor, none of us. You'se knows us," whined one of the men.

"Yes, and I know enough to send you all to Atlanta or Sing Sing or Danamora, for the rest of your rotten lives, if I want to."

The rascals stared vainly into the black vacuum of the screen, blinking in the glaring lights, cowering instinctively before the unseen but certain malignancy of the power behind that mysterious wall.

"I brought you here to New York," continued the master, "you are making more money with less work and risk than ever before. But you're playing false with me, and I know some one is slipping information where it oughtn't to go. I'm going to skin alive the one who I catch. There's one eye that never sleeps, don't forget that."

"Gee, boss, wot do we know to slip?" advanced the most forward of them. "We follers orders, and gets our kale and dat's all. We ain't never even seen ya, and don't know even wot de whole game is. Don't queer us, gov'nor!"

"Go out front again, and shut off this blab. I warn you that's all-Now, Phil, give this to the men. Tell them to keep off the cocaine - they're getting to be a lot of bone heads lately. Too much dope will spoil the best crook in the world."

The white hand passed out a roll of crisp, new currency to the lieutenant of the gang, who gingerly reached for it, as though he expected the tapering fingers to claw him.

"Fifty dollars to each man. No holding out. Remember, every one of them is spying on the other to me. I'm not a Rip Van Winkle. Now, I want you to keep this fellow Montague Shirley covered but don't put him away until I give you the word. Send the bunch upstairs, for I don't want to be disturbed the next two hours. And just keep off the coke yourself. You're scratching your face a good deal these days - I know the signs."

Phil expostulated nervously. "Oh, gov'nor, I ain't no fiend - just once and a while I gets a little rummy, and brightens up. It takes too much money to git it now, anyway. Goodbye, chief."

As he closed the wooden door to pay the gangsters, there was a slight grating noise, which followed a double click. A bar of wood automatically slid down into position behind the door, blocking a possible opening from the front of the cellar. The lights suddenly were darkened. The sound of shuffling feet would have indicated to a listener that the owner of the nervous hand was retreating to the rear of the darkened den. A noise resembling that of the turn of a rusty hinge might have then been heard: there was a metallic clang, the rattle of a sliding chain and the rear room was as empty as it was black!

In the front room, after payment from the red-headed ruffian,

Phil, the men clambered in single file up a wooden ladder to the street level. A trap-door was put into place and closed. Then the men began to shoot "craps" for a readjustment of the spoils, with the result that Red Phil, as his henchmen called him, was the smiling possessor of most of the money, without the erstwhile necessity of "holding out."

Then the gangsters scattered to the nearby gin-shops to while away the time before darkness should call for their evil activities. It was a cheerful little assortment of desperadoes, yet in appearance they did not differ from most of the habitués of New York garages, those cesspools of urban criminality.

From his club, Shirley telephoned Jim Merrivale in his down-town office, purposely giving another name, as he addressed his friend - a pseudonym upon which they had agreed during the night call. Shirley was suspicious of all telephones, by this time, and his guarded inquiry gave no possible clue to a wiretapping eavesdropper.

"How is the new bull-dog?" was the question, after the first guarded greeting. "Is he still muzzled?"

"Yes, Mr. Smith," responded Merrivale, "and the meanest specimen I have ever seen outside a Zoo! When I sent the groom out to feed him this morning, he snarled and tried to claw him. He's on a hunger strike. I looked up the license number on his collar but he's not registered in this state." (This, Shirley knew, meant the automobile tag under the machine which had been captured.)

"When are you apt to send for him - I don't think I'll keep him any longer than I can help."

"I'll send out from the dog store, with a letter signed by me. Feed him a little croton oil to cure his disposition. Good-bye, for now, Jim. I'll write you, this day."

Shirley hung up, and smiled with satisfaction at the news. The man would be glad to get bread and water, before long, he felt assured. However, he despatched a note to Cleary, of the Holland Agency, enclosing a written order to Merrivale to deliver over the prisoner, for safer keeping in the city.

This disposed of the started out from the club house for his afternoon of dissipation. As he left the doorway, he noticed the two men with the black caps standing not far away. They were engrossed in the rolling of cigarettes, but the swift glance which they shot at him did not escape Monty.

"Like the poor and the bill collectors, they are always with us," was his thought, as he calmly strolled over to the Hotel California. He determined to place them in a quiet, sheltered retreat at the earliest opportunity. He found Helene more attractive than ever.

"Shall I put on this wretched rouge again to-day," was the plaintive question, after the first greeting. "I hate it so - and yet, will do whatever you order."

"Your role calls for it, my dear girl. Perhaps we may close the dramatic engagement sooner than we expect. To-night should be an eventful one, for I will accept every lead which Reginald Warren offers. I would like to have a record of his voice, and that of some of his friends. There is a difference between the telephone voice and that heard face to face, - you would be a good witness if I could persuade him to sing or speak for me into a record. You can straighten out the difficulties of this case, if you will, in a thoroughly feminine manner."

"And what, sir, is that, I pray you?"

"Give him the opportunity - to fall in love with you."

Helene's cheeks flushed a stronger carmine than the rouge which she was administering, as she looked up in quick embarrassment.

"I don't want him to love me. I want no man to love me," was the petulant answer.

"Doubtless you have reason to be satisfied as things are," replied Shirley, puffing a cigarette, "but the softness of cerebral conditions increases in direct ratio with the mushiness of the affections. If it is important to us - and you are my partner in this fascinating business venture - will you not sacrifice your emotions to that extent: merely to let him lead himself on, as most men do?" He paused for a critical observation of her, and then added: "You are even more beautiful to-day than you were yesterday. He cannot help loving you if he is given the chance!"

Helene's white fingers crushed the orchid which she was pinning to the bosom of her gown. Her intent gaze met the mask of Shirley's ingenuous smile, reading in his telltale eyes a message which needed no court interpreter! Quickly she turned to her mirror to put the finishing touches to her coiffure, the golden curls so alluringly wilful.

"Your flattery, sir, is very cruel. Beware! I may take it seriously. What would happen if my verdant heart were to fall a victim to the cunning wiles of the voice? Remember, I have only met two men, since I came to America, yesterday. And they are both pronounced woman-haters. I will take you at your word, about Mr. Reginald Warren, and loosen my blandishments to the best of my rustic ability."

A wayward twinkle in her eyes should have warned Shirley that she was planning a little mischief. But, he was too preoccupied in finding the real front of her baffling street cloak to observe it. They left for the tearoom, while Helene still laughed to herself over certain subtle possibilities which she saw in the situation.

CHAPTER XIV

A PILGRIMAGE INTO FRIVOLITY

Rather early, again, for the usual throng, they were able to choose their position to their liking: to-day, it was in the center of the big room, close by the space cleared for the dancing. Gradually the tables were occupied, apparently by the identical people of the afternoon before, so marked is the peculiar character of the dance-mad individuality. To-day he varied his menu with a mild order of cocktails - for now he was not emulating the Epicurean record of the bibulous Grimsby. They observed with amusement the weird contortions, seldom graced by a vestige of rhythm or beauty, with which the intent dancers spun and zigzagged.

"Considering how much money they pay to learn these steps from dancing-masters, there is unusually small value in the market, Miss Marigold. I resigned myself to the approach of the sunset years, and became a voluntary exile in the garden of the wallflowers, when society dancing became mathematical."

"I don't understand?"

"Once it was possible to chat, to smile, to woo or to silently enjoy the music and the measures of the dance in company with a sympathetic partner. Now, however, since the triumph of the 'New Mode,' one must count 'one-two-three,' and one's partner is more captious than a schoolmarm! What puzzles me is the need for new steps, to be learned from expensive

Eustace Hale Ball

teachers, when it's so easy to slide down hill in this part of New York. But here endeth the sermon, for I recognize the amiable Pinkie at that other table, where she is studying your face with the malevolence of a cobra."

Helene slowly turned her eyes toward the other girl, who now advanced with forced effusiveness.

"Oh, my dear, and you're back again today. But where is dear old Grimmie; he is a nice old soul, though a trifle near-sighted. He wasn't half seas over last night - he was a war-zone submarine, out for a long-distance record!"

She impudently seated herself at the table with them, sending a questioning glance at the handsome companion of her quondam rival. Helene instinctively drew back, but a warning glance from Shirley plunged her into her assumed character, and she greeted the other girl with the quasi-comradeship of their class.

"Oh, yes, dear. Grimsby was a little poisoned by the salad or something like that: he was actually disagreeable with me, of all people in the world. But, I have so many friends that Grimsby does not give me any worry. He means nothing in my life. You seemed quite worried over him, though - "

"Yes, girlie," was Pinkie's effort to parry. "I was upset - not because he was with you, but to see the old chap showing his age. His taste has deteriorated so much since he started wearing glasses. But why don't you introduce me to your gentleman friend?"

Helene's faint smile expressed volumes, as she turned toward the modest Shirley with a bow of condescension. "This is Pinkie, one of old Grimsby's sweethearts, Mr. Shirley. I'm sure you'll like her."

"Are you Montague Shirley?" demanded the auburn-haired coquette with sudden interest. As Shirley nodded, she caught his hand with an ardent glance, ogling him impressively, as she continued: "I've heard a lot of you. I'm just that pleased to meet you!"

An indefinable resentment crept over Helene. How could this creature of the demi-monde have even distant acquaintance of such a wholesome, superior man as her escort? The effusiveness was irritating, and the overacted kittenishness of the girl made her sick at heart, although she betrayed no sign of her feeling. Helene could not understand that despite its mammoth size, New York is relatively provincial in the club and theatrical community, his acquaintanceship numbering into the thousands. Town Topics, the social gossipers of the newspapers and talkative club men bandied names about in such wise that it was easy for members of Pinkie's profession to satisfy their hopeful curiosity - prompted by visions of eventual social conquest on the one hand and a professional desire to memorize street numbers on the Wealth Highway for ultimate financial manipulations. As one of the richest members of the exclusive bachelor set, Montague Shirley, even unknown to himself, occupied reserved niches in the ambitions of a hundred and one fair plotters!

"You will honor us by taking a drink, Miss Pinkie?" was the criminologist's courteous overture.

"Pinkie Marlowe, if you want to know the rest of my name. Yes, I need a little absinthe to wake me up, for I just finished breakfast. We had a large party last night at Reg Warren's. Why don't you dance with me?"

"The old adage about fat men never being loved applies especially to those who brave the terrors of the fox-trot. I weigh two hundred, so I wisely sit under the trees and laugh at the others."

"You two hundred?" and admiration flashed from Pinkie's emotional eyes, "I don't believe it. Why, you're just right! I could dance with a man like you all night!"

Helene's helplessness only fanned the flames of her inward fury at the brazen intent of the girl. She forgot about Jack and even her plans about Reginald Warren. But Shirley's purpose was now rewarded, for Pinkie acted as the magnet to draw over several of the gilded youths whom they had met the day before. More introductions followed, and additional refreshments were soon gracing the table. Shine Taylor was the next to join the party, and erelong the waited-for visitor was approaching them. His eyes were upon Shirley from the instant that he entered the room: he advanced directly toward their table with a certainty which proved to Monty that method was in every move.

"What a pleasant surprise, little Bonbon!" exclaimed this gentleman as he drew up to their table. "I'm so glad. I was afraid you wouldn't get home safely with Grimsby; he was so absolutely overcome last night. He promised to bring you to my little entertainment but didn't show up. What became of him?"

"Join us in a drink and forget him," suggested Helene, as she took his hand with an innocently stupid smile. "This is Mr. Shirley, Mr. - Mr. - I had so much champagne last night I forgot your name."

"Warren, that's simple enough. Glad to see you, Mr. Sherwood, oh, Shirley! It seems as though I had heard your name - aren't you an actor, or an artist? A musician, or something like that? My memory is so miserable."

"I'm just a 'something like that,' not even an actor," was the answer, as the tiniest of nudges registered Helene's appreciation. "What is your favorite poison?"

Warren gave him a startled look, and then laughed: "Oh, you mean to drink? Now you must join me for I am the intruder." He drew out a roll of money; more nice, new hundred dollar bills.

Shirley remembered that old Van Cleft had drawn several thousand dollars from his office the night of the murder. Even his trained stoicism rebelled at thought of drinking a cocktail bought with this bloody currency!

"You didn't tell me about Grimsby?" persisted Warren, turning to Helene, with an admiring scrutiny of the girl's charms. "I'm rather interested."

"You'll have to ask him, not me. After we took a taxi from the Winter-Garden we had a ride in the Park. So stupid, I thought, at this time of the year. When I woke up, Grimmie was helping me into the entrance of the hotel. He was very cross with the chauffeur and with me, too. Then he took the taxi and went home, still angry."

"So!" after a moment's silence, Warren continued, a puzzled look on his face. "What was the trouble? I don't see how any one could be cross with a nice little girl like you. But to-night, I'm to have another little party up at my house. Bring some one up, who won't be cross. You come, Mr. Shirley?"

Helene hesitated, but Monty acquiesced.

"That would be splendid. What time?"

"About eleven. I'll expect you - I must run along now, as I'm ordering some fancy dishes."

Shirley had paid his waiter, and he rose with Helene.

"We must be leaving, too. I'll accept your invitation."

"And I'll be there, too, Mr. Shirley," put in Pinkie Marlowe. "I'll teach you some new steps. Reggie has a wonderful phonograph for dancing, with all the new tunes. See you later, girlie."

They were accompanied to the door by Shine and Warren. At

the check-room, Shirley was interested to note that Shine Taylor took out his green velour hat. His feet were adorned with white spats. After the door of their taxi had slammed he confided to Helene that he had located the gentleman who had caused his wreck that morning. Still, however, the clues were too weak for action. The car went first to the club, where Shirley sent in for any possible letters or messages. The servant brought out a note. It was another surprise. He gave an address to the driver and as the car turned up Fifth Avenue, he studied this missive with knit brows.

"A new worry?" asked Helene. "May I help you?"

He handed her the letter, and she noticed the nervous handwriting. It was short.

"Dear Mr. Shirley: Just received a threatening note demanding money. Can you come up at once? Howard V. C."

Shirley answered the question in the blue eyes, as she finished.

"As I thought it would turn out. Baffled in their game of robbing old men who have all left the city, they have begun to work the chance for blackmail. I will advise Van Cleft to pay them, and then we will follow the money. Here is the mansion and I will be out in five minutes."

He soon disappeared behind the bronze door. True to his promise, in five minutes he had returned. He looked up and down the Avenue amazed. Not a trace of the taxicab, nor of Helene Marigold could be seen!

Shirley's impulse was to pinch himself to awaken from the chimera. He knew she was armed, and would use the weapon if only to call for help. For the first time in his career the chill of terror crept into his heart - not for himself, but an irresistible dread of some impending danger for this unfathomable woman who had shared his dangers so uncomplainingly during this last wonderful day. He racked his mind vainly for some plausible reason. "She knows I need her. Yet at the supreme moment of the game she disappears. Can she be like other women, when she is most necessary?"

And he walked slowly down the Avenue, disconcerted, endeavoring to solve this sudden abortion of his best laid plans.

CHAPTER XV

CONCERNING HELENE'S FINESSE

Shirley endured a miserable three hours, in his attempts to locate the girl. She had not returned to the Hotel California, and he returned to the club in moody reflection. It was beginning to snow, and the ground was soon covered with a thin coat of white, through which he noticed his footprints stenciled against the black of the wet pavement. He wasted a dozen matches in the freshening wind, as he tried to light a cigarette. He stepped into a doorway on the Avenue to avail himself of its shelter. As he turned out to the street again, he almost bumped into two men, wearing black caps! One of them grunted a curt apology, as he stepped on.

"They are after me as usual," he thought. "Why not reverse operations and find out where they belong?"

It seemed hopeless: as in a checker game they had him at disadvantage with the odd number of the "move." Theirs was the chance to observe, and an open attempt to follow them would be ridiculous. Then, the footprints gave him an idea.

Dimly behind could be discerned the two men, as he quickened his pace, turning into a side street, off Fifth Avenue. Here he knew that traffic would be light, and his footprints the best evidence of his progress. The men unwittingly caught his plan, and dropped almost out of sight. At the intersection of Madison Avenue, they quickened their steps, and caught up with him again. Across corners, down quiet streets, and by purposed diagonals he led them: still they dogged his footprints. So adroit were they that only one experienced in the art could have realized their watchfulness.

Shirley now turned a corner quickly, into an unusually deserted thoroughfare, running with short steps, so as not to betray his speed by the tracks. Before they had time to round the corner he ran up the thinly blanketed steps of a private residence. Then he backed, as swiftly down the stoop, and thus crablike, walked across the street, down a dozen houses and backward still, up the steps of another private dwelling. Inside the vestibule he hid himself. The entry had strong wooden outside doors, and he tried the strength of the hinges: they satisfied him. A dim light burned behind the glass of the inner portal. He quietly clambered up the door, and balanced himself on the wood which gallantly stood the strain. Fortunately it did not come within four feet of the high ceiling of the old fashioned house.

He suffered a good ten minutes' wait before his ruse was rewarded. Being on the "fence" was a pastime compared to this precarious test of his muscles. The two men who had followed the first footprints tired of waiting before the house. One of them determined to investigate the other steps, which led into the house of their vigilance, from the other dwelling. And so he followed on, to the vestibule where he rang the bell. Shirley could have touched his head, so near he was, but the darkness of the upper space covered the retreat of the criminologist.

"What do you want?" was the angry question of an indignant old caretaker who answered the bell tardily. "You woke me up."

"Say, lady, can I speak to Mr. Montague Shirley?" began the man, gingerly.

"You get away from this house, you loafer or I'll call the police. No one by that name ain't here. Now, you get!"

She slammed the door in his face.

"I'll get Chuck to watch de udder joint," muttered the man, in a tone audible to Shirley. "Den I'll go back and git orders from Phil."

This habit of thinking aloud was expensive. Shirley stiffly but noiselessly slid down the steps, as he disappeared in the thickening snowfall. The criminologist slowly crossed the street, and sheltered himself in a basement entrance, from which he reversed the shadowing process. The twain hesitated before the first house, then one came up the sidewalk, as the other stood his ground. This man passed within a few feet of Shirley, who followed him over to Madison Avenue, then north to Fifty-fifth Street. Here he turned west, and turned into one of the old stables, formerly used by the gentry of the exclusive section for their blooded steeds. Into one building, which announced its identity as "Garage" with its glittering electric sign, the man disappeared.

Shirley paused, looked about him, and chuckled. For he knew that through the block on Fifty-sixth Street was the tall apartment building, known as the Somerset - the address given him by Reginald Warren.

"If I only had some word from Helene Marigold I could go ahead before they realized my knowledge."

Even as this thought crossed his mind, he turned back into Sixth Avenue. A hatless, breathless young person, running down the snowy street collided with him. As he began to apologize, he awoke to the startling fact that it was his assistant.

"Great Scott! What are you doing here? Where have you been all this time?"

The girl caught his arm unsteadily, but there was a triumph in her voice, as she cried: "Oh, this wonderful chance meeting. I was running down to my hotel but you have saved the day. I will tell you later. Quick, take this book."

She drew forth a volume, flexibly bound, like a small loose-leaf ledger. Shirley stuck it into his overcoat pocket, which he was already slipping about the girl's shivering shoulders.

"Take me back at once, for there is more for me to do."

"Where, my dear girl? You are indeed the lady of mysteries."

"To the basement of Warren's apartment house. I came down the dumb-waiter, when they left me. I left the little door ajar - Can you pull me up again? He is on the eighth floor. It is a long pull - Oh, if we can only make it before they return."

Her eyes sparkled with the thrill of the mad game, as she ran once more, Shirley keeping pace with her. The flurries of the snowstorm protected them from too-curious observation, as the streets seemed deserted by pedestrians who feared the growing blizzard. She led him to the tradesman's entrance of the Somerset, into the dark corridor through which she had emerged.

"Don't strike a light, for I can feel the way. We mustn't be seen."

Shirley obeyed, - at last she found the base of the dumbwaiter shaft.

"How did you have the strength to lower yourself down this shaft - it is no small task?" and his tone was admiring.

"I am not a weakling - tennis, boating, swimming were all in my education; they helped. But it is beyond me to pull all those floors, and lift my weight. Pull up as far as the little elevator car goes, then go away and come to his party to look for me. Do not be surprised at my actions. My role has really developed into that of an emotional heavy."

She patted his hand with a relaxation of tenderness, as he began to draw on the long rope. The girl was by no means a light weight, but at last the dumb-waiter came to a stop. Shirley heard the opening and closing of a door above. Then, still wondering at it all, he returned to the street as unobserved as they had entered. There was at least an hour to wait. He walked over to the Athletic Club, of which he was a remiss member, attending seldom during the recent months when his exercise had been more tragic than gymnastic work. In the library of the club house he sat down to study the volume which Helene had thrust into his hands at their startling meeting.

He gave a low whistle of surprise.

"Some little book!" he muttered, "and Helene Marigold has shown me that I must fight hard to equal her in the race for laurels!"

Then he proceeded to rack his brains with a new and knottier problem than any which he had yet encountered.

CHAPTER XVI

THE STRANGE AND SURPRISING WARREN

The volume was a loose-leaf diary, with each page dated, and of letter size. It covered more than the current year, however, running back for nearly eighteen months. It was as scrupulously edited as a lawyer's engagement book, and curiously enough it was entirely written in typewriting!

Most surprising of all, however, was the curious code in which the entire matter was transcribed, - the most unusual one which Shirley had ever read.

Here was the first page to which he opened, letter for letter and symbol for symbol:

"THURSDAY: JANUARY SEVENTH, 1915.
;rstmrfagtp,ansmlafrav;rudyrtaftreadocayjpi
dsmfaoma,ptmomha,pmlassdohmrfaypayscoae
ptlagptayrsadjomrasddohmrfagocahrmrsypta
,sthoragsotgscafsyraeoyjafrav;rudyrtasyagobra
djomrasmfalprajse;ruavobrtomhas,rakslras
smffanrmasddohmrfan;svlavstagpta,raqsofaqj
o;apmrajimftrfavpbrtomhadqrvos; aeptlakpn
agomodjrfatobrtdofraftobrasyarohjyoayjotfad
ocadjstqafrqpdoyr famohjyasmfaffuagpitayjpi
dsmfadsgrafrqpdoyagogyrrmajimftrfa; rmyaf
p;;ua,stopmayepajimfrtgptaftrddagptaqstyua
eoyjabsmv;rgyamrcyasgyrtmppmasfbsmvrfad

jomrapmrayjpidsm daypavpbrtapqyopmapga
usvjyadimnrs, aqsofaypantplrtayjsyamohjyapt
frfaqtpbodop,dayr;rqjpmragptausvjyayepa,p
myjabtiodra, pmlasddohmrdagptkpnamrcyafs
uasfbs mvrfadjomragojimftrfapmasvvpimyae
ptlapmaer;;omhypmadrtts;a,syyrtatrqsitdan;
svla,svjomra"

and so it ran on, baffling and inspiring a headache!

Shirley went over and over the lines of this bewildering
phalanx of letters with no reward for his absorbed devotion to
the puzzle.

"Let me see," he mused. "Thursday, January seventh, was the
date upon which Washington Serral was murdered, according
to Doctor MacDonald. Any man who will maintain a record
of the days in such a difficult code as this must not only be
extremely methodical, but is certain to have much to put upon
that record worth the trouble. Here may lay the secret of the
entire case."

At the end of the hour he had allowed himself, there was no
more proximity to solution than at the inception of his effort.
It was almost half-past eleven, and he knew that it was time to
go to Warren's apartment. He sent a messenger with the book,
carefully wrapped up, to his rooms at the club on Forty-fourth
Street. It was too interesting a document to risk taking up to
that apartment again, after Helene's exertions in obtaining it.

The Somerset was not dissimilar from the hundreds of highly
embellished dwellings of the sort which abound in the region
of the Park, causing out-of-town visitors to marvel justly at the
source of the vast sums of money with which to pay the
enormous rentals of them all.

The elevator operator smirked knowingly, when he asked for
Warren's apartment. "You-all can go right up, boss. He's
holdin' forth for another of dem high sassiety shindigs

to-night. Dat gemman alluz has too many callin' to bother with the telephone when he has a party. You don't need no announcin'."

The man directed him to the door on the left. Closed as it was the sounds of merrymaking emanated into the corridor. Shirley's pressure on the bell was answered by Shine Taylor's startled face. Warren stood behind him. The surprise of the pair amused Shirley, but their composure bespoke trained self-control.

"I'm sorry to be late," was the criminologist's greeting. "But I came up to apologize for not being able to bring Miss Marigold. We missed connections somewhere, and I couldn't find her."

"I am so pleased to have you with us anyway. We'll try to get along without her - " but Warren was interrupted to his discomfiture.

A silvery laugh came from the hallway behind him. Helene Marigold waved a champagne glass at Shirley.

"There's my tardy escort now. I'm here, Shirley old top! Te, he! You see I played a little joke on you this afternoon and eloped with a handsomer man than you." She leaned unsteadily against the door post and waved a white hand at him as she coaxed. "Come on in, old dear, and don't be cross now with your little Bonbon Tootems!"

Taylor and Warren exchanged glances, for this was an unexpected sally. But they were prompt in their effusive cordiality, as they assisted Shirley in removing his overcoat, and hanging his hat with those of the other guests. He placed his cane against the hall tree, and followed his host into the jollified apartment. He did not overlook the swift glide of Shine's hand into each of his overcoat pockets in the brief interval. Here was a skilful "dip" - Shirley, however, had taken care that the pickpocket would find nothing to worry him in the overcoat.

Warren's establishment was a gorgeous one. To Shirley it was hard to harmonize the character of the man as he had already deduced it with the evident passion for the beautiful. That such a connoisseur of art objects could harbor in so broad and cultured a mind the machinations of such infamy seemed almost incredible. The riddle was not new with Reginald Warren's case: for morals and "culture" have shown their sociological, economic and even diplomatic independence of each other from the time when the memory of man runneth not!

Shirley's admiration was shrewdly sensed by his host. So after a tactful introduction to the self-absorbed merrymakers, now in all stages of stimulated exuberance, he conducted his guest on a tour of inspection about his rooms.

"So, you like etchings? I want you to see my five Whistlers. Here is my Fritz Thaulow, and there is my Corot. This crayon by Von Lenbach is a favorite of mine." His black eyes sparkled with pride as he pointed out one gem after another in this veritable storehouse of artistic surprises. Few of the jolly throng gave evidence of appreciating them: the man was curiously superior to his associations in education as well as the patent evidence which Shirley now observed of being to the manor born. Helene Marigold, ensconced in a big library chair, her feet curled under her, pink fingers supporting the oval chin, dreamily watched Shirley's absorption. She seemed almost asleep, but her mind drank in each mood that fired the criminologist's face, as he thoroughly relaxed from his usual bland superiority of mien, to revel in the treasures.

Ivory masterpieces, Hindu carvings, bronzes, landscapes, rare wood-cuts, water colors - such a harmonious variety he had seldom seen in any private collection. The library was another thesaurus: rich bindings encased volumes worthy of their garb. The books, furthermore, showed the mellowing evidence of frequent use; here was no patron of the instalment editions-de-luxe!

"You like my things," and Warren's voice purred almost happily. There was a softening change in his attitude, which Shirley understood. The appreciation of a fellow worshiper warmed his heart. "My books - all bound privately, you know, for I hate shop bindings. Most of them from second-hand stalls, redolent with the personalities of half a hundred readers. Books are so much more worth reading when they have been read and read again. Don't you think so?"

"Yes. I see your tastes run to the modern school. Individualism, even morbidity: Spencer, Nietsche, Schopenhauer, Tolstoi, Kropotkin, Gorky - They express your thoughts collectively?"

"Yes, but not radically enough. My entire intellectual life has driven me forward - I am a disciple of the absolute freedom, the divinity of self, and - but there I invited you to a joy party, not a university seminar."

"But the party will grow riper with age," and Shirley was prone to continue the autopsy. "You are a university man. Where did you study?"

"Sipping here and there," and a forgivable vanity lightened Warren's face. "Gottingen, Warsaw, Jena, Oxford, Milan, The Sorbonne and even at Heidelberg, the jolly old place. You see my scar?" He pulled back a lock of his wavy black hair from the left temple to show a cut from a student duelist's sword. "But you Americans - I mean, we Americans - we have such opportunities to pick up the best things from the rest of the world."

"No, Warren," and Shirley shook his head, not overlooking the slight break which indicated that his host was a foreigner, despite the quick change. "I have been to busy wasting time to collect anything but fleeting memories. Too much polo, swimming, yachting, golfing - I have fallen into evil ways. I think your example may reform me. You must dine with me at my club some day, and give me some hints about making such wonderful purchases."

"I know the most wonderful antique shop," Warren began, and just then was interrupted by Shine Taylor and a dizzy blonde person with whom he maxixed through the Hindu draperies, each deftly balancing a champagne glass.

"Here, Reg, you neglect your other guests. Come on in!" Shine's companion held out a wine glass to Warren, but her eyes were fixed in a fascinated stare upon Montague Shirley,

"Why, what are you doing here?"

It was little Dolly Marion, Van Cleft's companion on the fatal automobile ride. She trembled: the glass fell to the floor with a tinkly crash. Shirley smiled indulgently. Taylor and Warren exchanged looks, but Monty knew that they must by this time be aware of his command to the girl to abstain from gay associations.

"You couldn't resist the call of the wild, could you, Miss Dolly?"

The girl sheepishly giggled, and danced out of the room, to sink into a chair, wondering what this visitation meant. Another masculine butterfly pressed more champagne upon her, and in a few moments she had forgotten to worry about anything more important than the laws of gravity. Warren had been rudely dragged away from his intellectual kinship with his guest. His manner changed, almost indefinably, but Shirley understood. He looked at Helene, a little bundle of sleepy sweetness in the big chair.

"Well, Miss! Where did you go when I left you on my call of condolence to Howard Van Cleft? He leaves town to-night for a trip on his yacht, and it was my last chance to say good-bye."

"Where is he going?" was Warren's lapsus linguae, at this bit of news.

"Down to the Gulf, I believe. Do you know him, Warren? Nice chap. Too bad about his father's sudden death from heart failure, wasn't it? He told me they were putting in supplies for a two months' cruise and would not be able to sail before three in the morning."

"I don't know Van Cleft," was Warren's guarded reply. "Of course, I read of his sad loss. But he is so rich now that he can wipe out his grief with a change of scene and part of the inheritance. It's being done in society, these days."

"Poor Van Cleft! He's besieged by blackmailers, who threaten to lay bare his father's extravagant innuendos, unless he pays fifty thousand dollars. He can afford it, but as he says, it's war times and money is scarce as brunette chorus girls. He has put the matter before the District Attorney and is going to sail for Far Cathay until they round up the gang. These criminals are so clumsy nowadays, I imagine it will be an easy task, don't you, Warren?"

The other man's eyes narrowed to black slits as he studied the childlike expression of Shirley's face. He wondered if there could be a covert threat in this innocent confidence. He answered laconically: "Oh, I suppose so. We read about crooks in the magazines and then see their capers in the motion picture thrillers, but down in real life, we find them a sordid, unimaginative lot of rogues."

He proffered Shirley a cigarette from his jeweled case. As he leaned toward the table to draw a match from the small bronze holder, Helene observed Shirley deftly substitute it for one of his own, secreting the first.

"Yes," continued Shirley, "the criminal who is caught generally loses his game because he is mechanical and ungifted with talent. But think of the criminals who have yet to be captured - the brilliant, the inspired ones, the chess-players of wickedness who love their game and play it with the finesse of experts."

Shirley smoothed away the ripple of suspicion which he had mischievously aroused with, "So, that is why fellows like us would not bother with the life. The same physical and intellectual effort expended by a criminal genius would bring him money and power with no clutching legal hand to fear. But there, we're getting morbid. What I really want to do is to satisfy my vanity. Where did Miss Marigold disappear?"

"Talking about me?" and Helene opened her eyes languorously. "I was so tired waiting for you that when Mr. Warren came along in his wonderful new car I yielded to his invitation, so we enjoyed that tea-room trip which you had promised. Such a lark! Then we came up here where I had the most wonderful dinner with him and three girls. I was tired and sleepy, so I dozed away on that library davenport until the party began - and there you are and here I are, and so, forgive me, Monty?"

She slipped nimbly to the floor, with a maddening display of a silken ankle, advancing to the criminologist with a wistful playfulness which brought a flush of sudden feeling, to the face of Reginald Warren. Helene was carrying out his directions to the letter, Shirley observed.

They lingered at Warren's festivities until a wee sma' hour, Helene pretending to share the conviviality, while actually maintaining a hawk-like watch upon the two conspirators as she now felt them to be. She was amused by the frequency with which Shine Taylor and Reginald Warren plied their guest with cigarettes: Shirley's legerdemain in substituting them was worthy of the vaudeville stage.

"The wine and my smoking have made me drowsy," he told her, with no effort at concealment. "We must get home or I'll fall asleep myself."

A covert smile flitted across Warren's pale face, as Shirley unconventionally indulged in several semi-polite yawns, nodding a bit, as well. Helene accepted glass after glass of wine, thoughtfully poured out by her host. And as thoughtfully, did she pour it into the flower vases when his back was turned: she matched the other girls' acute transports of vinous joy without an error. Shirley walked to the window, asking if he might open it for a little fresh air. Warren nodded smiling.

"You are well on the way to heaven in this altitude of eight stories," volunteered Shirley, with a sleepy laugh.

"Yes. The eighth and top floor. A burglar could make a good haul of my collection, except that I have the window to the fire escape barred from the inside, around the corner facing to the north. Here, I am safe from molestation."

"A great view of the Park - what a fine library for real reading; and I see you have a typewriter - the same make I used to thump, when I did newspaper work - a Remwood. Let me see some of your literary work, sometime - "

Warren waved a deprecating hand. "Very little - editors do not like it. I do better with an adding machine down on Wall Street than a typewriter. But let us join the others." There was a noticeable reluctance about dwelling upon the typewriter subject. Warren hurried into the drawing-room, as Shirley followed with a perceptible stagger.

Shine Taylor scrutinized his condition, as he asked for another cigarette. As he yielded to an apparent craving for sleep, the others danced and chatted, while Taylor disappeared through the hall door. After a few minutes he returned to grimace slightly at Warren. Shirley roused himself from his stupor.

"Bonbon, let us be going. Good-night, everybody."

He walked unsteadily to the door, amid a chorus of noisy farewells, with Helene unsteady and hilarious behind him. Warren and Shine seemed satisfied with their hospitable endeavors, as they bade good-night. The elevator brought up two belated guests, the roseate Pinkie and a colorless youth.

"Oh, are you going, Mr. Shirley? What a blooming shame. I just left the most wonderful supper-party at the Claridge to see you."

"Too bad: I hope for better luck next time."

"The elevator is waiting," and Helene's gaze was scornful. Shirley restrained his smile at the girl's covert hatred of the redhaired charmer. Then he asked maliciously: "Isn't she interesting? Too bad she associates with her inferiors."

"You put it mildly."

"Here, boy, call a taxicab," he ordered the attendant, as they reached the lower level.

"Sorry, boss, but I dassent leave the elevator at this time of night. I'm the only one in the place jest now."

Shirley insisted, with a duty soother of silver, but the Negro returned in a few minutes, shaking his head. Shirley ordered him to telephone the nearest hacking-stand. Then followed another delay, without result.

"Come, Miss Helene, there is method in this. Let us walk, as it seems to have been planned we should."

"Is it wise? Why put yourself in their net?"

For reply, he placed in her hand the walking stick which he had so carefully guarded when they entered the apartment. It was heavier than a policeman's nightstick. As he retook it, she observed the straightening line of his lips.

"As the French say, 'We shall see what we shall see.' Please walk a little behind me, so that my right arm may be free."

It was after two, and the street was dark. Shirley had noted an arc-light on the corner when he had entered the building -

now it was extinguished. A man lurched forward as they turned into Sixth Avenue, his eyes covered by a dark cap.

"Say gent! Give a guy that's down an' out the price of a beef stew? I got three pennies an' two more'll fix me."

"No!"

"Aw, gent, have a heart!" The man was persistent, drawing closer, as Shirley walked an with his companion, into the increasing darkness, away from the corner. Another figure appeared from a dark doorway.

"I'm broke too, Mister. Kin yer help a poor war refugee on a night like this?"

Shirley slipped his left hand inside his coat pocket and drew out a handkerchief to the surprise of the men. He suddenly drew Helene back against the wall, and stood between her and the two men.

"What do you thugs want?" snapped the criminologist, as he clenched the cane tightly and held the handkerchief in his left hand. There was no reply. The men realized that he knew their purpose - one dropped to a knee position as the other sprang forward. The famous football toe shot forward with more at stake than ever in the days when the grandstands screeched for a field goal. At the same instant he swung the loaded cane upon the shoulders of the upright man, missing his head.

The second man swung a blackjack.

The first, with a bleeding face staggered to his feet.

The handkerchief went up to the mouth of the active assailant, and to Helene's astonishment, he sank back with a moan. Shirley pounced upon his mate, and after a slight tussle, applied the handkerchief with the same benumbing effect. Then he rolled it up and tossed it far from him.

He took a police whistle from his pocket and blew it three times. His assailants lay quietly on the ground, so that when the officer arrived he found an immaculately garbed gentleman dusting off his coat shoulder, and looking at his watch.

"What is it, sir?" he cried.

"A couple of drunks attacked me, after I wouldn't give them a handout. Then they passed away. You won't need my complaint - look at them - "

The policeman shook the men, but they seemed helpless except to groan and hold their heads in mute agony, dull and apparently unaware of what was going on about them.

"Well, if you don't want to press the charge of assault?"

"No. I may have it looked up by my attorney. Tonight I do not care to take my wife to the stationhouse with me. They ought to get thirty days, at that."

Shirley took Helene's arm, and the officer nodded.

"I'll send for the wagon, sir. They're some pickled. Good-night."

As they walked up to the nearest car crossing, Helene turned to him with her surprise unabated.

"What did you do to them, Mr. Shirley?"

"Merely crushed a small vial of Amyl nitrite which I thoughtfully put in my handkerchief this afternoon. It is a chemical whose fumes are used for restoring people afflicted with heart failure: with men like these, and the amount of the liquid which I gave them for perfume, the result was the same as complete unconsciousness from drunkenness. - Science is a glorious thing, Miss Helene."

CHAPTER XVII

IN WHICH SHIRLEY SURPRISES HIMSELF

They reached the hotel without untoward adventure.

"Perhaps we might find a little corner in that dining-room I saw this afternoon, with an obliging waiter to bring us something to eat. Shall we try? I need a lot of coffee, for I am going down to the dock of the Yacht Club to await developments."

"You big silly boy," she cautioned, with a maternal note in her voice which was very sweet to bachelor ears from such a maiden mouth, "you must not let Nature snap. You have a wonderful physique but you must go home to bed."

"It can't be done - I want to hear about your little visit to the apartment, and the story of the diary. I'll ask the clerk."

A bill glided across the register of the hotel desk, and the greeter promised to attend to the club sandwiches himself. He led them to a cosey table, in the deserted room, and started out to send the bell-boy to a nearby lunchroom.

"Just a minute please, - if any one calls up Miss Marigold, don't let them know she has returned. I have something important to say, without interruption: you understand?"

"Yes, I get you, sir," and the droll part was that with a

familiarity generated of the hotel arts he did understand even better than Shirley or Helene. He had seen many other young millionaires and golden-haired actresses. Shirley looked across the table into the astral blue of those gorgeous eyes. Certain unbidden, foolish words strove to liberate themselves from his stubborn lips.

"I am a consummate idiot!" was all that escaped, and Helene looked her surprise.

"Why, have you made a mistake?"

"I hope not. But tell me of Warren's mistake."

She had been waiting what seemed an eternity before Van Cleft's house, when a big machine drew up alongside. Warren greeted her with a smiling invitation to leave Shirley guessing. Her willingness to go, she felt, would disarm his suspicions. The little dinner in the apartment with Shine, Warren and three girls had been in good taste enough: pretending, however, to be overcome with weariness she persuaded them to let her cuddle up on the couch, where she feigned sleep. Warren had tossed an overcoat over her and left the apartment with the others, promising to return in a few minutes. He had said to Shine, "She'll be quiet until we return - it may be a good alibi to have her here." Then he had disappeared, wearing only a soft hat, with no other overcoat. Listening at the closed hall door, she heard him direct the elevator man, "Second off, Joe." The door was locked from the outside. The servant's entrance was locked, all the bedrooms locked, every one with a Yale lock above the ordinary keyhole. The Chinese cook had been sent out sometime before to buy groceries and wine for the later party.

"But where did you find the note-book? It may send him to the electric chair." Monty Shirley was lighting one of the cigarettes handed him by his host. He sniffed at it and crushed out the embers at the end. "This cigarette would have sent me to dreamland for a day at least - Warren understands as much chemistry as I do."

"At first I studied the books in the library out of curiosity and then noticed that three books were shoved in, out of alignment with the others on the shelf. With a manservant in the house, instead of a woman, of course things needed dusting. But where these three books were it had been rubbed off! I took out the books, reached behind and found the little leather volume. It was simple. I went to his typewriter when I saw that the pages were all typed, and took out some note-paper, from the bronze rack."

"And then, Miss Sleuth?"

"Don't laugh at me. I had heard of the legal phrase 'corroborative evidence,' so knowing that it would be necessary to connect that typewriter with the book, I rattled off a few lines on the machine. Here it is: it will show the individuality of the machine to an expert."

"You wonderful girl!" he murmured simply. She protested, "Don't tease me. I have watched you and am learning some of your simple but complete methods of working. I understand you better than you think."

"Go on with your story," and Shirley was uncomfortable, although he knew not why.

"That is the end of my tale of woe. The kitchen being open, I took advantage of the dumb-waiter, as you already know. It's fortunate that waiter is dumb, for it must have many lurid confessions to make. I never saw such an interminable shaft; it seemed higher than the Eiffel Tower. See how I blistered my hands on the rope, letting myself down."

She opened her palms, showing the red souvenirs of the coarse strands. Almost unconsciously she placed her soft fingers within Shirley's for a brief instant. She quickly drew them away, sensing a blush beneath the cosmetics, glad that he could not detect it. That gentle contact thrilled Shirley again, even as the dear memory of the tired cheek against his shoulder, during the automobile trip of the previous night.

"After finding you so accidentally and returning with your aid, on the little elevator, I threw myself back into the original pose on the big couch. It was just in time, for Warren returned. His cook came in shortly afterward. I imagine that he allows no one in that apartment, ordinarily, when he is not there himself. But what, sir, do you think I discovered upon the shoulder of his coat?"

Shirley shook his head. "A beautiful crimson hair," he asked gravely, "from the sun-kissed forehead of the delectable Pinkie? Or was it white, from the tail of the snowy charger which tradition informs us always lurks in the vicinity of auburn-haired enchantresses?"

"Nothing so romantic. Just cobwebs! He saw me looking at them, and brushed them off very quickly."

"The man thinks he is a wine bottle of rare vintage!" observed Shirley. But the jest was only in his words. He looked at her seriously and then rapt in thought, closed his eyes the better to aid his mental calculation. "He got off at the second floor - He wore no overcoat - A black silk handkerchief - cobwebs - and that garage on the other street, through the block! Miss Helene, you are a splendid ally!"

"Won't you tell me what you mean about the garage? Who were those men who attacked you? What happened since I deserted you?"

But Shirley provokingly shook his head, as he drew out his watch.

"It is half-past two. I must hurry down to East Twenty-fifth Street and the East River, at the yacht club mooring, before three. Tomorrow I will give you my version in some quiet restaurant, far from the gadding crowd of the White Light district."

He rose, drawing back his chair; they walked to the elevator together. The clerk beckoned politely.

"A gent named Mr. Warren telephoned to ask if you were home yet, Miss Marigold. I told him not yet. Was that wrong?"

"It was very kind of you. Thank you so much," and Helene's smile was the cause of an uneasy flutter in the breast of the blasé clerk. "Good-night."

"That's a lucky guy, at that, Jimmie," confided the clerk to the bell-boy. "She is some beauty show, ain't she? And she's on the right track, too."

"Yep, but she's too polite to be a great actress or a star. Her temper'ment ain't mean enough!" responded this Solomon in brass buttons. "I hopes we gits invited to the wedding!"

Outside, Shirley enjoyed the stimulus of the bracing early morning air. A new inspiration seemed to fire him, altogether dissimilar to the glow which he was wont to feel when plunging into a dangerous phase of a professional case. He slowly drew from his pocket the typed note-paper which had nestled in such enviable intimacy with that courageous heart. The faint fragrance of her exquisite flesh clung to it still. He held it to his lips and kissed it. Then he stopped, to turn about and look upward at the tall hostelry behind him. High up below the renaissance cornice he beheld the lights glow forth in the rooms which he knew were Helene's.

As he hurried to the club, he muttered angrily to himself: "I have made one discovery, at least, in this unusual exploit. I find that I have lost what common sense I possessed when I became a Freshman at college!"

CHAPTER XVIII

ON THE RISING TIDE

A hurried message to the Holland Agency brought four plain clothes men from the private reserve, under the leadership of superintendent Cleary. Monty met them at the doorway of the club house, wearing a rough and tumble suit.

They sped downtown, toward the East River, the criminologist on the seat where he could direct the driver. At Twenty-sixth Street, near the docks, they dismounted and Shirley gave his directions to the detectives.

"I want you to slide along these doorways, working yourselves separately down the water front until you are opposite the yacht club landing. I will work on an independent line. You must get busy when I shoot, yell or whistle, - I can't tell which. As the popular song goes, 'You're here and I'm here, so what do we care?' This is a chance for the Holland Agency to get a great story in the papers for saving young Van Cleft from the kidnappers."

He left them at the corner, and crossing to the other pavement, began to stagger aimlessly down the street, looking for all the world like a longshoreman returning home from a bacchanalian celebration from some nearby Snug Harbor. It was a familiar type of pedestrian in this neighborhood at this time of the morning.

"That guy's a cool one, Mike," said Cleary to one of his men. "These college ginks ain't so bad at that when you get to know 'em with their dress-suits off."

"He's a reg'lar feller, that's all," was Mike's philosophical response. "Edjication couldn't kill it in 'im."

A hundred yards offshore was the beautiful steam yacht of the Van Clefts', the "White Swan." Lights on the deck and a few glowing portholes showed unusual activity aboard. Shirley's hint to Warren about the contemplated trip to southern climes was the exact truth. Naked truth, he had found, was ofttimes a more valuable artifice than Munchausen artistry of the most consummate craft! The longshoreman, apparently befuddled in his bearings, wandered toward the dock, which protruded into the river, a part of the club property. He staggered, tumbled and lay prostrate on the snowy planks.

Then he crawled awkwardly toward one of the big spiles at the side of the structure, where he passed into a profound slumber. This, too, was a conventional procedure for the neighborhood! A man walked across the street, from the darkness of a deserted hallway: he gave the somnolent one a kick. The longshoreman grunted, rolled over, and continued to snore obliviously.

An automobile honk-honked up Twenty-third Street, and then swung around in a swift curve toward the dock. The investigating kicker slunk away, down the street. The limousine drew up at the entrance to the tender gangway. Accompanied by a portly servant, a young man in a fur coat, stepped from the machine.

"Give them another call with your horn, Sam," he directed. "The boat will be in for me, then."

This was done. A scraping noise came from the hanging stairway of the dock, and a voice called up from the darkness: "Here we are, sir!" Howard Van Cleft leaned over the edge and looked down, somewhat nervously. A reassuring word came up

Eustace Hale Ball

from the boat, rocking against the spiles.

"You was a bit late, sir. You said three, Mr. Van Cleft, and now it's ten after. So the captain sent us in to wait for you. Everything's shipshape, sir, steam up, and all the supplies aboard. Climb right down the ladder, sir. Steady now, lads!"

This seemed to presage good. Van Cleft turned to his butler.

"Take down the luggage, Edward. Goodbye, Sam. Keep an eye on the machines. The folks will attend to everything for you while I am away. Good-bye."

The butler had delivered the baggage and now returned up the ladder, puffing with his exertions.

"Good-bye, sir," and his voice was more emotional than usual. "Watch yourself, sir, if you please, sir. You're the last Van Cleft, and we need you, sir." The old man touched his hat, and climbed into the automobile, as Van Cleft climbed down the ladder. The machine sped away under the skilful guidance of Sam.

"Steady, sir, steady - There, we have you now, sir, - Quick, men! Up the river with the tide. Row like hell! - Keep your oars muffled - here comes the other boat."

All this seemed naturally the accompaniment of the embarkment of Van Cleft's yachting cruise, but the sleeping longshoreman suddenly arose to his feet and blew a shrill police whistle. Next instant the flash of his pocket-lamp illumined the dark boat below him. A volley of curses greeted this untoward action! A revolver barked from the hand of a big man in the stern. Young Van Cleft lay face downward in the boat, neatly gagged and bound. As the light still flickered over the surprised oarsmen, an answering shot evidenced better aim. The man in the back of the bobbing vessel groaned as he fell forward upon the prostrate body of the pinioned millionaire. One oarsman disappeared over the side of the boat, to glide into the unfathomable darkness, with skilful strokes.

"Hold still! I'll kill the first man who makes a move!"

As Shirley's voice rang out, Cleary with his assistants was dashing across the open space to the end of the dock.

"Shove out that boat-hook and hold onto the dock!" was the additional order, accompanied by a punctuation mark in the form of another bullet which splintered the gunwale of the boat. Looking as they were, into the dazzling eye of the bulb light, the men were uncertain of the number of their assailants: surrender was natural. Cleary's men made quick work of them. The boat from the yacht now hove to by this time, filled with excited and profane sailormen. The skipper of the "White Swan," revolver drawn, stood in its bow as it bumped against the stairway. Howard Van Cleft was unbound: dazed but happy he tried to talk.

"What - why - who?" he mumbled.

"Pat Cleary, from the Holland Detective Agency," was Shirley's response. "There, handcuff these men quick. Two cops are coming. We want the credit of this job before the rookies beat us to it."

Van Cleft recognized the speaker, and caught his hand fervently. Shirley, though, was too busy for gratitude. He gave another quick direction.

"Hurry on board your yacht tender and get underway. Your life isn't worth a penny if you stay in town another hour. These men will be attended to. Good luck and goodbye."

The young man rapidly transferred his luggage to his own boat. They were soon out of view on their way to the larger vessel. Shirley turned toward Cleary.

"I'll file the charge against these two men. They tried to rob me and make their getaway in this boat. You were down here as a bodyguard for Van Cleft, who, of course, knew nothing about the matter as he left for his cruise. So his name can be kept out of it entirely. And the fact that you helped to save him from paying fifty thousand dollars in blackmail, will not injure the size of Captain Cronin's bill. Get me?"

"It's got!" laughed Cleary.

Two patrolmen were dumfounded when they reached the spot to find four men in handcuffs in charge of six armed guardians. The superintendent explained the situation as laid out by Shirley. The cavalcade took its way to the East Twenty-first Street Police Station, where the complaint was filed. Sullen and perplexed about their failure, the men were all locked in their cells, after their leader had his shoulder dressed by an interne summoned from the nearby Bellevue Hospital.

Shirley and Cleary returned with the others to the waiting automobile, after these formalities. The prisoners had been given the customary opportunity to telephone to friends, but strangely enough did not avail themselves of it.

"We're cutting down the ranks of the enemy, Cleary," observed the detective as he lit a cigarette. "But I wonder who it was that escaped in the water?"

"He'll be next in the net. But say, Mr. Shirley, what percentage do you get for all this work, I'm awondering?" was the answering query. The criminologist laughed.

"Thanks, my dear man, simply thanks. That's a rare thing for a well-to-do man to get since the I.W.W. proved to the world that it's a crime for a man to own more than ten dollars, or even to earn it! But I wish you would drop me off about half a block from the Somerset Apartments, on Fifty-sixth Street. I want to watch for a late arrival."

He waited in the shadows of the houses on the opposite side of the street. After half an hour he was rewarded by the sight of Mr. Shine Taylor dismounting from a taxicab. The young gentleman wore a heavy overcoat over a bedraggled suit. One of his snowy spats was missing; his hat was dripping, still, from its early immersion. He entered the building, after a cautious survey of the deserted street, with a stiff and exhausted gait.

Shirley was satisfied with this new knot in the string. He returned to his rooms at the club, to gain fresh strength for the trailing on the morrow. And this time, he felt that he deserved his rest!

Next morning, after his usual plunge and rub-down, he ordered breakfast in his rooms. He instructed the clerk to send up a Remwood typewriter, and began his experiments with the code of the diary.

From an old note-book, in which were tabulated the order of letter recurrences according to their frequency in ordinary English words, he freshened his memory. This was the natural sequence, in direct ratio to the use of the letters: "E: T: A: O: N: I: S: B: M, etc." The use of "E" was double that of any other. Yet on the pages of the book he found that the most frequently recurring symbol was "R" which was, ordinarily, one of the least used in the alphabet. "T," which would have been second in popularity, naturally, was seen only a few times in proportion. "Y," also seldom used, appeared very often. The symbol "A" was used with surprising frequency.

"Let me see," he mused. "This code is strictly typewritten. It must be arranged on some mechanical twist of the typing method. A is used so many times that it might be safe to assume that it is used for a space, as all the words in this code run together. If A is used that way, what takes its place? S would by rights be seventh on the list, but the average I have made shows that it is about third or fourth."

Carefully he jotted down in separate columns on a piece of paper the individual repetitions of letters on the page of

"January 7, 1915." He arrived at the conclusion, then, that "R" was used for "E," that "S" took the place of "A" and that "Y" alternated in this cipher for "T" which was second on his little list.

Fur the benefit of the reader who may be interested enough to work out this little problem, along the lines of Shirley's deductions the arrangement of the so-called "Standard" keyboard is here shown, as it was on the "Number Four" machine of Warren's Remwood, and the duplicate machine which Shirley was using.

QWERTYUIOP

ASDFGHJKL;

ZXCVBNM,.

Shift SPACE BAR   Shift
Key   Key

This diagram represents the "lower case" or small letters, capitals being made by holding down one of the shift keys on either side, and striking the other letter at the same time, there being two symbols on each metal type key. As only small letters were used through the code Shirley did not bother about the capitals. He realized at last, that if his theory of substitution were correct the writer had struck the key to the right of the three frequent letters. He had the inception of the scheme.

Starting with the first line of the sentences so jumbled on the page for January 7, 1915, he began to reverse the operation, copying it off, hitting on the typewriter the keyboard letter to the left of the one indicated in the order of the cipher.

The result was gratifying. He continued for several lines, having trouble only with the letter "P." At last he realized that the only substitution for that could be "Q." In other words,

"A" had been used for the space letter throughout, and for all the other symbols the one on the right had been struck, except "P" which being at the end of the line had been merely swung to the first letter on the other end of it!

No wonder Warren had been so confident of its baffling simplicity! Many of the well-known rules for reading codes would not work with this one, and had it not been for Shirley's suspicion, aroused in the library of the arch-schemer the night before, he would hardly have given the typewriter, as a mechanical aide, a second thought. Warren's desire to drop the subject of machines had planted a dangerous seed.

Laboriously Shirley typed off the material of the entire page for the fatal Thursday, and his elation knew no bounds as he realized that here was a key to many of the activities of his enemy. He donned his hat and coat and hurried over to the Hotel California to show his discovery to Helene. She invited him up to her suite at once, where he wasted no words but exhibited the triumphant result of his efforts. He handed her his own transcription, and this is what she read:

"January 7, 1915, Thursday.

learned from bank de cleyster drew six thousand in morning monk assigned to taxi work for tea shine assigned to fix generator margie fairfax date with de cleyster at five, shine and joe hawley covering game jake and ben assigned black car for me paid phil one hundred covering special work job finished riverside drive at eighty third sharp deposited night and day four thousand safe deposit fifteen hundred lent dolly marion two hundred for dress for party with van cleft next afternoon advanced shine one thousand to cover option of yacht sunbeam paid to broker that night ordered provisions telephone for yacht two month cruise monk assigned for job next day advanced shine five hundred on account work on wellington serral matter repairs black machine fifty party apartment same night champagne one hundred fifty caterer one hundred tips fifty five to janitor taxis twelve must stir phil up on work for grimsby matter memorandum arrange for yacht mooring on east river instead of north after Wednesday eighth job finis memorandum settle telephone exchange proceeds not later than monday paid electrician special wiring two hundred in full settlement."

"There, Miss Helene, how do you like my little game of letter building?"

There was a boyish gleam of triumph in his smile as he turned toward her.

"You are a wizard, but how did you work it all out?" There was no smile in her face, only a mingled horror at the revelations of this calculating monster in his businesslike murder work, and an unfeigned admiration for Shirley's keenness.

"A very old method, but one which would have availed for naught without your help. The letter paper which you used and the unmistakable identity of Warren's machine are two more bars of iron with which to imprison him. The paper of that note is the same on which they wrote to Van Ceft for money, and their threats to me. This shows from a microscopic examination of its texture. I will give the whole book to a trustworthy stenographer: more than six months of these little confessions are tabulated here. Warren was evidently so used to this code that he could write in it as easily as I do with the straight alphabet. His training in German universities developed a thoroughness, a methodical recording of every thing, which is apt to cost him dearly. And his undoubted vanity prompted him to have a little volume of his own in that library to which he could turn occasionally for the retrospection of his own cleverness. Now, I must investigate this clever telephone system. I think I have the clue necessary."

He intrusted the book to Helene for the morning, promising to return in an hour or two with new information, drolly refusing to tell her his destination.

"You're a bad, bold boy, and should be spanked, for not letting some one know where to look for you in case you get into difficulties," she pouted. "Perhaps I will do some equally foolish thing myself."

"If you knew how you frightened me yesterday!" he began.

"Did you really worry and really care?" But Shirley had slipped out of the door, leaving her to wonder, and then begin that long delayed letter to Jack.

CHAPTER XIX

AN EXPEDITION UNDERGROUND

The criminologist picked his way through the swarming vehicles which swung up and down Broadway, across to Seventh Avenue, where he turned into a plumber's shop. This fellow had handled small jobs on Shirley's extensive real estate holdings, and he was naturally delighted to do a favor in the hope of obtaining new work.

"Mike, I want to borrow an old pair of overalls, a jumper and one of those blue caps hanging up on your wall. And I need some plumbers' tools, as well, for a little joke I am to play on one of my friends."

The workman was astounded at such a request from his rich client, but nodded willingly. The dirtiest of the clothes answered Shirley's requirements and with soot rubbed over his face and hands, his hair disarranged, he satisfied his artistic craving for detail. He was transformed into a typical leadpipe brigand. Hanging his own garments in the closet, after transferring his automatic revolver into the pocket of the jeans, he started out, carrying the furnace pot, and looking like a union-label article.

He reached the Somerset by a roundabout walk, passing more than one of his acquaintances with inward amusement at their failure to recognize him. He had arranged for Helene to invite Shine Taylor and Reginald Warren down to call on her at the apartment in the California at this particular time. So thus he felt that the coast was clear. At the tradesmen's entrance, where he had gone before to hoist on the dumbwaiter, he entered the building. An investigation of the basement showed him that in the rear of the building were one large and two small courts or air shafts. Then he ascended the iron stairway to the street level of the vestibule.

"Say, bo, I come to fix de pipes on de second floor," was his self-introduction to the haughty negro attendant. "Dey're leakin' an' me boss tells me to git on de job in a hustle."

"Which one? I ain't heard o' no leaks. It must be in de empty apartment in de rear, kase dat old maid in de front would been kickin' my fool head off ef she's had any trouble. She's always grouchy."

"Sure, dingy, it's de empty one in de rear. Lemme in an' I'll fix it."

"You-all better see de superintendent. People is apt to be lookin' at dat apartment to-day to rent it, an' he mightn't want no plumber mussin' round. I'll go hunt 'im fer you-all."

"Say, you jest lemme in now. I'm paid by de hour. You knows what plumber bills is, an' your superintendent'll fire you if he has to pay ten dollars' overtime 'cause you hold me up."

This was superior logic. The negro took him up and opened the door. Shirley entered, and peered out of the court window in the rear. Helene's suggestion about the dust was applicable here, for he found all the windows coated except the one opening upon the areaway. Below he observed a stone paving with a cracked surface. It was semidark, but his electric pocket-light enabled him to observe one piece of the rock which seemed entirely detached. Shirley investigated the closets of the empty apartment. In one of them he discovered the object of his search. It was a knotted rope. He first observed the exact way in which it had been folded in order to replace it without suspicion being aroused. Then he took it to the small window of the air shafts hanging it on a hook which was half concealed behind the ledge. Down this he lowered himself, hand over hand. The stone was quickly lifted - it was hinged on the under surface. n the dark hole which was before him there was an iron ladder. Down he went, into the utter blackness. His outstretched hands apprised him that he was at the beginning of a walled tunnel, through which he groped in a half-upright position. He reached an iron door, and remembering his direction calculated that this must be at the rear entrance of the old garage on West Fifty-fifth Street. It opened, as he swung a heavy iron bar, fitted with a curious mechanism resembling the front of a safe. Softly he entered, carrying his heavy boots in his hand. All was still within, and he shot the glow ray of his little lamp about him. As the reader may guess, it was the rear room of Warren's private spider-web! The table, facing the screen was surmounted by an ingenious telephone switchboard.

Shirley examined this closely. The various plugs were labelled: "Rector," "Flatbush," "Jersey City," "Main," "Morningside," and other names which Shirley recognized as "central" stations of the telephone company. Here was the partial solution of the mysterious calls. He determined to test the service!

He took up the telephone receiver and sent the plug into the orifice under the label, "Co." wondering what that might be. Soon there was an answer.

"Yes, Chief. What is it?"

"How's everything?" was Shirley's hoarse remark. "I find connections bad in the Bronx? What's the matter?"

"I'll send one of the outside men up there to see, Chief. There's a new exchange manager there, and he may be having the wires inspected. But my tap is on the cable behind the building. I don't see how he could get wise."

Shirley smiled at this inadvertent betrayal of the system: wire tapping with science. He was able to trap the confederate with his own mesh of copper now.

"I want to see you right away. Some cash for you. I'm sick with a cold in the throat so don't keep me waiting. Go up town and stand in the doorway at 192 West Forty-first Street. Don't let anybody see you while you wait there, so keep back out of sight. How soon can you be there?"

"Oh, in half an hour if I hurry. Any trouble? You certainly have a bum voice, Chief. But how will I know it's you?"

"I'll just say, 'Telephone,' and then you come right along with me, to a place I have in mind. Don't be late, now! Good-bye."

Shirley drew out the connection and tried the exchange labeled "Rector." Instantly a pleasant girl's voice inquired the number desired.

"Bryant 4802-R."

This was the Hotel California.

The operator on the switchboard of the hostelry replied.

"Give me Miss Marigold's apartment, please."

Helene's voice was soon on the wire. Shirley asked for Warren in a gruff tone.

"What do you want?" was that gentleman's musical inquiry, in the tones which were already so familiar to the criminologist.

"Chief, dis is de Rat. I wants to meet you down at de Blue Goose on Water Street in half an hour. Kin you'se come? It's important."

The other was evidently mystified.

"The Rat? What do you mean? I don't know you. Ring off!"

Shirley heard the other receiver click. He held the wire, reasoning out the method of the intriguer. Soon there was a buzz in his ear, and Warren's voice came to him. It was droll, this reversal of the original method, which had been so puzzling.

"What number is this?"

"Rector 4471, sir," answered the criminologist in the best falsetto tone he could muster. Then he disconnected with a smile. This was turning the tables with a vengeance. But he knew that he must be getting away from the den before the possible investigation by Warren or his lieutenant. There were many things he would have liked to study about the place. But his curiosity about the telephone had made it impossible for him to remain. It was a costly mistake, as events were destined to prove!

He hurried out of the compartment, into the tunnel, up the rope and through the window. He replaced the knotted rope, exactly as it had been before. He put a few drippings of molten lead from the bubbling pot, under the wash-stand of the bathroom, to carry out the illusion of his work as plumber. Then he departed from the building, as he had entered.

In ten minutes he was changing his garments in Mike's plumbing shop, with a fabulous story of the excruciating joke he had played upon a sick friend. Then he walked rapidly to the doorway at 192 West Forty-first Street.

Back against the wall of this empty store entry, lounged a pleasant-looking young man who puffed at a perfecto. Shirley stepped in, and in a low tone, said: "Telephone." The other started visibly, and scrutinized the well-groomed club man from head to foot.

"Well, Chief, you're a surprise. I never thought you looked like that. Where will we go?"

"Over to the gambling house a friend of mine runs, just around the corner. There we can talk in quiet."

Shirley led the way, restraining the smile which itched to betray his enjoyment of the situation. The other studied him with sidelong glances of unabated astonishment. They were soon going up the steps of the Holland Agency, which looked for all the world, with its closed shutters, and quiet front, like a retreat for the worshipers of Dame Fortune. Cronin fortunately did not believe in signs. So the young man was not suspicious, even when Shirley gave three knocks upon the door, to be admitted by the sharp-nosed guardian of the portal.

"Tell Cleary to come downstairs, Nick," said the criminologist. "I want him to meet a friend of mine."

The superintendent was soon speeding two steps at a time.

"The Captain is back, Mr. Shirley," he exclaimed. "He's in the private office on a couch."

"Good, then we'll take my friend right to him."

The stranger was beginning to evidence uneasiness, and he turned questioningly to his conductor, with a growing frown.

"Say, what are you leading me into, Chief?"

Shirley said nothing but strode to the rear of the floor, through the door of Captain Cronin's sanctum. The old detective was covered with a steamer shawl, as he stretched out on a davenport. The young man observed the photographs around the room, - an enormous collection of double-portraits of profile and front face views - the advertized crooks for whom Cronin had his nets spread in a dozen cases. The handcuffs on the desk, the measuring stand, the Bertillon instruments on the table, all these aroused his suspicions instantly.

He whirled about, angrily.

Shirley smiled in his face. Then he addressed the surprised Captain Cronin.

"Here is our little telephone expert who arranged the wires for Warren and his gang, Captain. You are welcome to add him to your growing collection of prisoners."

For answer the young man whipped out a revolver and fired point-blank at the criminologist. His was a ready trigger finger. But he was no swifter than the convalescent detective on the couch, who had swung a six shooter from a mysterious fold of the steamer blanket, and planted a bullet into the man's shoulder from the rear.

As the smoke cleared away, Shirley straightened up from the crouching position on the floor which had saved him from the assassin, and dragged the wounded criminal to his feet. The handcuffs clicked about his wrists before the young man had grasped the entire situation. Cleary and three others of the private force were in the room.

"I've got to hurry along now, Captain. Just let him know that his Chief is captured and the sooner he turns State's evidence the better it will be for him. The District Attorney might make it lighter, if he helps. I'll be back this evening if I can." And Shirley hurried away, leaving much surprise and bewilderment in every mind.

Cronin was equal to the task of picking up the threads, and under his sarcasm, and Cleary's rough arguments, the prisoner admitted some interesting matters about the mysterious employer whose face he had never seen. But Shirley's task was far from completed.

CHAPTER XX

A DOUBLE ON THE TRAIL

Shirley walked up to the Hotel California, at the door of which he met Warren and Taylor just leaving. They looked some-what embarrassed but his manner was cordiality itself.

"Sorry you are going. I was just stepping up to see Miss Marigold. Won't you come back?"

His invitation was refused. Then Shirley urged Warren to be his guest at the club for dinner that evening. This was accepted with a surprising alacrity. So, he left them, and was soon talking with Helene.

"You missed a curious little sociable party," she assured him. "They tried to quiz me, and I confess that I worked for the same purpose - no results on either side. But, Warren had an unusual telephone call, which disturbed him so much that he hurried away, sooner than he had planned."

Shirley recounted his explorations of the afternoon, with the explanation of Reginald's disturbance. It was certain now that the leader of the assassins had something to cause uneasiness, - enough to take his mind off the campaign of murder and blackmail.

"But he will try to get you out of the way," was her anxious answer. "You are multiplying needless dangers. Why don't you have him arrested now - the phonograph records will identify his voice, will they not? The diary will show his career, and everything seems complete in the case."

Shirley sat down in the window-seat, before replying.

"It is just my own vanity, then, perhaps. I am foolish enough to believe that I can trap him on some crime which will give him the complete punishment he deserves without dragging in the names of these unfortunate old society men. All our trouble would be for nothing, just now, if the story came out. The phonograph records helped me - but I prefer to keep that method to myself, as a matter of interest and selfishness. Somewhere, in that beautiful apartment of his there must be clues which will send him to the electric chair on former crimes: Warren is an artist who has handled other brushes than the ones he used on this masterpiece. He is not a beginner. So, I must ransack his apartment."

"That is impossible, with all the care he takes with bolts and locks."

"We shall see. Meanwhile, I'll spin the yarn of the last thirty-six hours. I'm sure your curiosity is whetted: my own is by no means satisfied."

So he gave her a survey of the progress he had made. Helene brought forth a number of typewritten pages which she had transcribed from the diary, proudly exhibiting a machine which she had ordered sent up from the hotel office.

"There, sir, we are unwinding the ravelings of his past life to an extent. I have found a mysterious reference to a Montfluery case in Paris, during August of last year. What can you do to investigate that lead?"

Shirley jotted down the name, and answered: "A cable to the prefecture of Police of the city of Paris from Captain Cronin will bring details. That should be an added link in the chain, within the next twenty-four hours. I am going to leave you for the while, as I wish to investigate a certain yacht which is moored in the East River. That yacht is there for a purpose - you remember his reference to the payment of supplies for a two-month cruise. My amateurish vanity leads me to a hope that I can capture him just at the crucial moment when he thinks he is successful in his escape from pursuit."

"That is the childishness of the masculine mind," retorted Helene. "You say we women are illogical, but we are essentially practical in the small things. I would advise closing the doors before the horse escapes, rather than a chase from behind!"

"Perhaps," answered Monty, "but the uncertainty does allure me. I always enjoyed skating on thin ice, from the days of college when I loved to get through a course of lectures on as little work as possible. The satisfaction of 'getting away with it' against odds was so exhilarating. I will return after my little dinner with Warren at the Club. Where will you dine?"

"Your friend Dick Holloway is taking me to some restaurant where singing and music may alter my refusal to him."

"Your refusal?" and Shirley shot a quick glance at the girl. Her dimples appeared as she added: "Yes - he wants me to star in a little play for the coming spring, but I have had such fun playing in real-life drama that I said him nay."

"Oh," was all the criminologist said, but as he left, Helene's laugh interpretated a little feminine satisfaction. Monty's mind was just disturbed enough about the attitude of Dick Holloway to keep him from worrying over the Warren case until he had reached the East River, near the yacht club mooring.

There was the white yacht which had been mentioned in the purloined book. It was a trim, speedy craft. The criminologist walked down a few blocks to the office of a boat contractor with whom he had dealt on bygone occasions.

"I want to engage a fast motor-boat, Mr. Manby," was his request. "The speediest thing you've got. Keep it down at your dock, at Twenty-first Street, with plenty of gasoline and a man on duty all the time, starting with six o'clock to-night. I may need it at a minute's notice."

"I've got a hydroplane which I'll sell this spring to some yachtsman," said Manby. "It's a bargain - you can do forty miles an hour in it, without getting a drop of spray. Shall I show it to you?"

"Yes, and the two men who you will have alternating on duty, so they will know me when I come for it. I'll pay for every minute it is reserved."

They soon came to terms; the men were introduced and Shirley was well satisfied with the racing craft, which was moored according to his directions, handy for a quick embarkation.

Then he went up to the Holland Agency. Cronin was disappointed in his results with the telephone confederate. All of Warren's men were close-mouthed, as though through some biting fear of swift and unerring vengeance for "squealing." Even the prisoners in the station-house had not volunteered to communicate with friends, as they were allowed to do by law. They were "standing pat," as the old detective declared in disgust.

"That proves one thing," remarked the criminologist. "They are not local products, or they would have friends other than their chief on whom to call for bail or aid. Their whole work centers on him. I think I will send a code message to this man Phil this afternoon or evening. He may be able to read it, and if he does, it may assist us. I wish you would have a man call on Miss Marigold at the California Hotel, so that she may know his face. Then keep him covering her for they are apt to get suspicious of her and try to quiet her. She is a game and fearless girl, but she is no match for this gang."

Cronin assigned one of the men immediately, and the sleuth took up a note of introduction to Helene, in which Monty explained the need for his watch.

Shirley then repaired to the club house to await his dinner guest. He was thoughtful about the alacrity of Warren to dine with him. There was more to this assumed friendliness than the mere desire to talk to him.

"I wonder if he wants to keep me occupied for some certain reason?" pondered the club man. "Helene is protected now by a silent watcher. The members of the Lobster Club are all out of the city. Van Cleft is safe on the ocean. They must be laying a trap. I wonder where that trap would be?"

As he looked about his rooms he realized that many important pieces of evidence were locked up in his chests and the small safe. His bedroom, in the uppermost floor of the club building, was in a quiet and less frequented part of the house. Shirley summoned one of the shrewd Japanese valets who worked on the dormitory floors of the building.

"Chen," he began. "Are you a good fighter?"

The Mongolian grinned characteristically. Shirley took out a bill, and handed it to the little fellow.

"I have reason to think some one may come into my rooms to-night, while I am busy downstairs. How would you like to lock yourself on the inside of my clothes closet, and wait? The air is not very good, but with this ten dollars you could take a nice ride in the country to-morrow, and get lots of good oxygen in your lungs to make up for it."

Chen was a willing little self-jailer. Shirley handed him his own revolver, and the slant eyes sparkled with glee at the opportunity for some excitement. Americans may carp at the curious manners and alleged shortcomings of the Oriental, but personal fear does not seem to be in the category of their faults.

So, with this little valet, who improved his time, as Shirley had discovered, by taking special courses in Columbia University's scientific department. The criminologist had used him on more than one occasion when Eastern subtlety and apparent lack of guile had accomplished the impossible!

The closet door was closed, and Shirley went downstairs. At the desk of the, club clerk he sent a cablegram to the police authorities of Paris. The message was simple

"Cable collect to Holland Detective Agency name and record of man in Montfleury case, August, 1914. Do you want him? .

.... Cronin, Captain."

Shirley smiled as he handed the envelope to the little messenger who had been summoned, and made his exit through the front doorway just as the affable Reginald Warren entered it: another instance of "ships that pass in the night," was the thought of the host who advanced courteously.

"You are on time to the minute: German training, I see. Let the boy have your hat and coat, Mr. Warren."

These little amenities completed, they sauntered about the beautiful building, Shirley pointing out the many interesting photographs of athletic teams, trophies, club posters, portraits of famous graduates, and the like, which seem part and parcel of collegiate atmosphere. Warren was profoundly interested, yet there was an abstraction in his conversation which was not unobserved by his entertainer. As they passed a tall, colonial clock in the broad hallway, Shirley caught him glancing uneasily at it. This was the second time he had looked at its silvered face since they came into the range of it. Purposely the club man took him down the length of the big dining-hall, to exhibit the trophies of the hunt, from jungles and polar regions, contributed by the sportsmen members of past classes. Here Shirley chatted about this and that boar's head, yonder elephant hide, the other tiger skin, until he had consumed additional time. As they passed into the lounging room Shirley led his guest past another small mahogany clock. Again the sharp, anxious glance at the progress of the minutes. He was convinced by now that some deviltry was being perfected on schedule time. He began to worry over his little assistant on the floor high above: perhaps he would not be able to cope with the plotters, after all. Yet, Chen was wiry, cunning, and needed no diagrams as to the purpose for which he was to guard the rooms.

At last Shirley led Warren to the grill-room where they ordered their dinner: the supreme test of a gentleman is his taste in the menu for a discriminating guest. Warren sensed this, as the delicious viands and rare old wines were brought out in a combination which would have warmed the heart cockles of the fussiest old gourmon from Goutville!

"Ah, a feast fit for the gods," were his admiring words, as the two men smiled across this strange board of hospitality. In the midst of the meal, their chat of student days was interrupted by a page who approached Shirley.

"Begging your pardon, sir, but I have a note which was left here by messenger for a gentleman named Mr. R. Warren; your guest, I believe, sir?"

Warren's face flushed, and his surprise was indubitable. He snatched the envelope from the boy, who had reached it toward Shirley. The criminologist was no less in the dark. Warren, with a scant apology, tore open the missive. It was typewritten! He read it, and his brows came together with an angry scowl.

He arose from his seat swiftly, turning toward Shirley with a nervous twitching of the erstwhile firm lips.

"Would you pardon me if I ran? A Wall Street client of mine has suddenly been stricken with apoplexy. We have deals together, dependent upon gentlemen's agreements, without a word of writing. It may mean a fortune to get to him before he loses all power of speech. It is a shame to spoil, at this time, such a wonderful dinner as I had promised myself with you. Can you forgive me?"

The man was visibly panic-stricken, although his superb nerve was fighting hard to cover his terror. Shirley wondered what news could have fallen into his hand this way. He watched the envelope, hoping that he would inadvertently drop it. But no such luck! Warren carefully folded it and put it with the letter into the breast pocket of his coat.

"My dear fellow, business before indigestion, always! I am sorry to have you go, but we will try again. I will go upstairs with you. Shall I call a taxicab for you?"

Warren expostulated, but the host followed him to the check room. Unseen by Warren, Shirley inserted a handkerchief from his own pocket into the overcoat pocket of the other with a sleight-of-hand substitution, in the withdrawal of the guest's small linen square!

Warren rushed to the door. He sprang into the first taxicab that came along, and disappeared. Shirley watched the car as it raced away and noticed its number. He turned to the door man.

"Whose machine was that? On the regular club stand here?"

"Yes, sir. A man named Perkins drives it, sir."

"Will it return here as soon as the fare is taken to the end of the trip?"

"Yes, sir, they have orders for that. They belong to a gent who supplies cars for our club exclusively, sir. They are not allowed to take outside passengers."

"Very good! You send for me, in my rooms, as soon as the

driver of the car shows up. I want to find out where he went."

Shirley hurried up in the lift to his own floor. He went to the door of his room, and tried to open it with his key. It was bolted from inside! There came a muffled report from within. Then he heard a cry, which he recognized as the voice of Chen, the Jap. He dropped to the floor, listening at the crack – a scuffle was in progress within!

Eustace Hale Ball

CHAPTER XXI

A BURGLARY FOR JUSTICE

Shirley rose, and once more applied that gridiron-trained boot of his: this time to the lock of the door. Two doses resulted in a complete cure for its obstinacy. As he rushed into the room, he saw a figure swing out of the window on a dangling rope. He hesitated - the desire to chase this intruder to the roof of the club struggled with his duty to the unfortunate Jap, who lay on the floor, where he was being garroted by a burly ruffian in a chauffeur's habiliments. He sprang toward his little assistant, and made quick work of the big man.

As he threw the other, with one of his "silencer" twists of the neck cords, the Jap sprang up. A demoniac anger twisted that usually smiling countenance, and it took all of Shirley's strength, to wrest away the automatic revolver from the maddened valet, to prevent swift revenge.

"Why, Chen. He's caught. Don't shoot him now!"

Chen, with a voluble stream of Nagasaki profanity, spluttered in `rage, and strove like a bantam rooster to get at his antagonist. The necessity for quieting him to prevent bloodshed was fatal to the pursuit of the other man, as Shirley realized bitterly. The servants were running to the room by this time. The club steward opened the battered door, and Shirley turned to explain.

"You have a brave little man, here, Cushman. Chen heard this burglar in my room, and tried to capture him at the risk of his own life. He deserves promotion and a raise in salary. Go downstairs and call the police. We'll have this fellow locked up!"

The man glared at Shirley, and rubbed his throat which throbbed from the vice-like grip of the jiu-jitsu. Chen still breathed hard and his almond eyes rolled nervously. At last he was quiet again, although the slender fingers twitched hungrily for a clawing of that dirty neck. Shirley patted him on the back. Judgment had come to another of the gangsters, and the criminologist was pleased at the diminution in the ranks of his opponent.

An examination of his cabinet and dresser drawers showed that the pillaging had barely begun when Chen popped out of his hiding-place. It was no wonder that Warren had been so solicitous as to the speeding time: intuition had once more intervened to interrupt these well-laid schemes.

The little Jap could tell barely more of his adventure than that he had opened the door when he heard men walking and talking in the room. Then the struggle had ensued, with the result already described.

Now, indeed, was Shirley more puzzled than ever at Warren's sudden departure. It had upset the plans of the conspirators: it was an unwelcome surprise to their Chief. And furthermore it had interfered with a little scheme of the criminologist by which he had expected to craftily imprison his guest for the remainder of the night.

The room was put in order - not much was there to rearrange, for the tussle had come so promptly. With a final look at his belongings, Shirley left Chen in charge, not forgetting to slip to him another reward for his courage.

Then he went downstairs and hurried over to the Hotel

Eustace Hale Ball

California to hold a conference of war with Helene Marigold.

She was nervous, as she greeted him. Yet a subtle smile on her face showed that she was not surprised by the visit. Shirley quickly outlined the occurrences of the dinner hour. When he asked her opinion, for he had learned to place a growing trust in her quick grasp of things, she walked silently to her typewriter.

"Here, sir, is a little note which may amuse you."

She handed him a piece of paper. It read:

"Chief: The Monk has turned up at the Blue Goose on Water Street. He is drunk and telling all he knows. Come down at once to help us quiet him. Hurry or every thing will be known. You know who."

Shirley looked at the message, and then with tilted eyebrows at his fair companion.

"What do you know about the Blue Goose?" he asked. "And the Monk? For I presume that you wrote this out?"

"Your presumption is correct. I remembered hearing Warren ask Taylor this afternoon after that telephone call from you, where the Blue Goose saloon could be. Taylor told him it was a sailor's dive on Water Street. The night they thought me dreaming on his library couch, I heard Taylor ask Warren if they had heard from the Monk. So, it seemed to me that the two questions might interest Mr. Reginald Warren if presented in a language that he understood."

"And what was that language?"

"It was a code message, which I typed out on this Remwood machine here, by the system you told me. It was slow work, but I finished it and sent it over to the club, knowing Warren would be with you. I really don't know what good the message would do. But being an illogical woman, and a descendant of Pandora, I thought it would be amusing to open the Pandora's box and let all the little devils loose, just to see the glitter of their wings!"

Shirley caught her hands delightedly.

"You bully girl! Nothing could have happened better. I'll improve my time now, by visiting Mr. Warren's apartment, impolite as it is without an invitation. And then I think I will go calling in that little cave of the winds in the rear of his art collection, on the other street."

"But, Monty - I Mean, Mr. Shirley," and a rosy embarrassment overcame her, "you will put your head into the lion's mouth once too often. Why not wait until you get him under lock and key?"

"My dear girl, we will telephone my club and talk to the door man. I think that he may be under lock and key by this time, in a manner you little suspect. Let me have the number."

He went to the instrument on her dressing-table. The club was soon reached, and Dan the door man was answering his eager question.

"Yes, sir, the taxi has come back, sir."

"Send the chauffeur to the wire. I want to talk to him," said Shirley. The man was soon speaking. "What address did you take that gentleman to, my man?"

"Why, sir, I started out for the Battery, but sir, a terrible thing happened."

"What was it?"

"The gentleman was overcome with an ep'leptic stroke or somethin' like that. He pounded on the winder behind me,

and when I stopped me car, and looked in he was down an'
out. I was on Thirty-third Street and Fift' Avenue at the time,
so I calls a cop, and he orders me to run 'im over to Bellevue.
He's there now, sir. He ain't hardly breathin', sir. It's terrible!"

"Too bad, I must go and call, to see if I can help him!" was
Shirley's remark as he hung up the receiver. He repeated the
news to Helene. Her eyes sparkled, as she said: "Ah, those
symptoms resemble the ones you told me which came from
that amo-amas-amat-citron, or whatever it was."

"Not quite such a loving lemon, Miss Marigold," he chuckled.
"Amyl nitrite. The same soothing syrup which quieted our
would-be robbers on Sixth Avenue, that night when we left his
apartment. It will wear off in about three hours. I had a little
glass container folded in my own handkerchief, which I put in
his overcoat pocket as a parting souvenir, crushing it as I did
so. I reasoned that undue anxiety which he displayed might
cause him to mop his brow, close to that student-duel scar.
One smell of the chemical on that handkerchief, in the
quantity which I gave, was enough to quiet his worries. Now
for the Somerset Apartment."

He looked at his watch.

"It is eight fifteen. I want you to telephone up to Warren's
apartment exactly at ten o'clock. Tell them - there should be a
them, that I have been overcome in your apartment, and that
they are the only people who can help you, or who know you.
I believe that the idea of finding me unconscious, and getting
me away will bring any and all of his friends who may be there.
If Taylor is there with others, he will hardly leave them in the
place when he goes. What I want is to be sure that the coast is
cleared of people at that hour. Then I will make an
investigation into his papers and other matters of interest. Can
I count on you?"

A reproachful pouting of the scarlet lips was the only answer.
Shirley left, this time hurrying uptown to a certain engine

-house, whose fire captain he had known quite well in the old reportorial days.

It was beginning to snow once more. And as Shirley slipped out of the engine-house, carrying a scaling ladder which he had borrowed after much persuasion from his good-natured friend, he thanked his luck for this natural veiling of the night, to baffle eyes too curious about the campaign he had planned. He knew the posts of the policemen on this street, and sedulously avoided them.

The Warren apartment faced the Eastern side of the structure, and when he reached the front of the Somerset, he sought for a way in which to use his implement. A scaling ladder, it may be explained to the uninitiated, is about eight feet long - a single fire-proof bar, on which are short cross-pieces. At one end is a curiously curving serrated hook, which is used for grappling on the sills of windows or ledges above. It is the most useful weapon for the city fire-fighter, enabling him to climb diagonally across the face of a threatened structure, or even to swing horizontally from one window to a far one, where ladders and hose-streams might not reach.

A hundred feet to the West of the Somerset he found the excavations for a new apartment house. No watchman was in sight, in the mist of falling flakes, so the criminologist disappeared over the fence which separated the plot of ground from the sidewalk. Advancing with many a stumble through the blasted rock and shale, he obtained ingress to an alleyway in the rear. Following this brought him to the back of the Somerset. Shirley had an obstinate grandfather, and heredity was strong upon him. It seemed a foolhardy attempt to scale the big structure, but he raised the ladder to the window-sill of the second story, climbing cautiously up to that ledge.

On the second sill he rested, then stretched his scaler diagonally forward to the left. As he put his feet upon this, he swung like a pendulum across the space. It was a severe grueling of nerves, but his judgment of placement was good.

When the ladder stopped swinging he clambered up another story, as he had learned to do on truant afternoons wasted at the firemen's training school, during the privileged days of journalistic work.

Floor after floor he ascended, until he reached the eighth, on which was Shirley's great goal. Here he exerted the utmost prudence, refraining from the natural impulse to look down at the great crevasse beneath him. His footing was slippery, but the thickening snowfall was a boon in white disguise, for it protected him from almost certain observation from the street below. Slowly he raised his eyes to a level with the illuminated window, and peered in.

A strange sight greeted him.

Shine Taylor was busily engaged in the 'twisting of coils of wire, about shiny brass cylinders, with an array of small and large clocks, electric batteries and mysterious bottles on the carved library table. He was intent upon the manufacture of another of his diabolical engines of death!

Even as he watched, the door opened and who should stagger into the room but Reginald Warren!

"Great Scott, Reg! What hit you?" was Taylor's ejaculation, as the other stumbled forward, with a hand to his purple face, to sink into an easy-chair, groaning. The man outside the window could not distinguish the words, but the current of thought was well expressed in pantomime.

"I've been drugged!" moaned Warren. "That devil put something on my handkerchief which knocked me out. I came to in Bellevue and I had a time getting away to come back here. What about the Monk? Did you see him?"

Taylor had run to his side. It seemed as though Warren's eyes would pop from his head. The veins were swollen on his pallid brow, and he gasped for air.

"Open the window!" he murmured, and his confederate rushed to the very portal through which the criminologist was watching this unusual scene, with bated breath. His heart sank, as he lowered himself with a suddenness which vibrated the loosely-attached scaler. For the first time his eyes turned toward the terrifying distance from which he had ascended.

There was a squeak and he heard the window slide in its frame. He felt that all was over. It would be impossible for Shine Taylor not to observe the hooked prong of the ladder, with its curving metal a few inches from his hands. In this ghastly minute of suspense, Shiley's thoughts, strangely enough turned back to one thing. He did not dash through the gamut of his life experiences nor regret all past peccadilloes, as novelists inform us is generally the ultimate thought in the supreme moment before a dash into eternity! He felt only a maddening, itchingly bewitching desire to reach up to his coat pocket and draw out that scent-laden page of typed note-paper which had been glorified by its caress of the warm, bare bosom of the wonderful woman who had so mysteriously drifted into the current of his life.

Then he heard a voice through the open window so close to his ears: it was Shine Taylor's nasal whine.

"It's snowing, Reg. The air will do you good. What a gorgeous night for a murder. Tell me now, what was the trouble?"

And Shirley swung, and swung and swung!

CHAPTER XXII

IN THE DOUBLE TRAP

Eternity had passed, the Judgment Day had been overlooked and new aeons had gone their way, it seemed to the criminologist, when the voice was audible again.

"Oh, all right. I just drew it down from the top. Tell me about your doping. Who was the devil?"

He had been unobserved. By the grace of the fates, Warren's sudden appearance had given him a better chance to hear their secrets, and Taylor's own abstraction had dissipated any interest in the world beyond the window. Again he lifted himself to the level of the sill, sure that the creamy curtains upon which the light from the big electrolier was beaming, would shield him from their view. Warren called for some brandy. Taylor served him, but it was three minutes or more before the other could collect himself. Then he began furiously, as the pain in his forehead diminished.

"This Shirley: he's a clever dog. He put something on my handkerchief, and when I got that message of yours it got me, right in the taxicab, as I was on my way to the Blue Goose to meet you."

"To meet me?" and Taylor's turn came to be startled. "I don't know why you should meet me at the Blue Goose!"

"Say, didn't you send me this note in code?" demanded Warren, drawing out the typewritten sheet. Taylor shook his head, with a blanched face.

The other looked at him with the first evidence of fear which Shirley had ever seen on the confident face. Warren caught his assistant's hand, and drew his face down toward the note.

"Look, it is in our code. Phil can read it but he is the only one beside you. He is locked up in jail, and couldn't reach a typewriter. I got a message from him this afternoon that he wouldn't squeal. You know how he smuggled it out to me. Tell me how could any one know about the Monk and write this so?"

Taylor shook his head, speechless. As he turned his face toward the window Shirley observed the great drawn shadows under his squinting eyes. The sudden shock was telling on that weasel face. Taylor walked unsteadily toward the infernal machine, and he looked blankly toward Warren again. The other's blazing orbs were full upon him now. There was a frightful menace in their glittering depths as he spoke.

"Taylor, if I thought you had sold out I'd skin you alive right now!"

"Reg - Reg - you are my best friend. Don't say a thing like that."

"Are you selling me for some purpose. Are you soft on that chicken? Has she blarneyed you into this?" demanded his chief, rising, unsteadily, but fierce in his suspicious tensity.

Taylor cowered, with imploring hands stretched out.

"Why, Reg, no one ever did for me what you've done. I'd die rather than sell you out, and there ain't a dame in the world that could make me soft on a real game like this."

As Warren studied his white face there came a tinkle on the telephone.

"What's that? Who's that?" Warren turned and ran toward the instrument, still studying the face of his companion. It was evident that a seed of distrust was planted in his bosom. He answered nervously.

"Yes, yes! What do you want? Who's speaking?"

Then he listened, and a wise expression came over his face. It broke into a smile for the first time since he entered the room. He winked at Taylor who drew near him. Shirley strained his ears to catch the words.

"Yes, yes, why, my dear Miss Bonbon. Surely, I'll be glad to come down - To help take care of Mr. Shirley - Of course, I will come in my machine and bring him uptown to a hospital - That's what you want? - Yes, indeed, nothing would give me greater pleasure."

He rang off, and turned toward Taylor.

"That smooth devil has sniffed some of his own dope as sure as you live, Shine. We'll get him. Call up and have the machine sent around. You and I will be a committee of two, and we'll end this tonight. Bring what you need."

Warren drank another full glass of brandy, while Taylor gave a quick order over the telephone. Then the latter snatched up a small black satchel which was standing on a side table. The assistant came to the window, and Shirley dropped down out of sight, for another moment of suspense. But the sash was quickly closed and bolted.

The light was turned out, and he waited another five minutes, stiffening in the cold wind which had sprung up to send the big flakes in eddies against his numbed fingers. With difficulty he fished out a long, thin wire from his pocket, with which he had frequently turned the safety catch of windows on other such occasions. Again it served its purpose, and he drew himself up to the sash of the opened window. He brushed off the snow, so as to leave no telltale puddles of drippings. He went to the door of the library, and then to that of the vestibule.

It was locked from the outside, even as they had done when Helene was the drowsy prisoner.

He had little time, he knew, for his search, but he first thought of the girl's predicament. He must cover the tracks there. He took up the receiver, and in a minute was talking to her.

"I'm in. Leave word downstairs (and pay the clerk and bell-boy a good bribe) that you have gone to a hospital with a sick friend. Tell them to swear to that, and better still leave the hotel at once, hunt up Dick Holloway - you'll find him at the Thespis Club to-night. Send in the chauffeur to ask for him and have him stay with you in the machine. I am going to visit the other place when I finish here. I'll be down there, at the Thespis Club, by eleven again. Good-bye - use your wits."

Then he began a hurried ransacking of the apartment. He picked up a note-book here, sheets of memoranda there, letters and documents which he thought would be convenient. Warren's bedrooms were locked, but a small "jimmie" sufficed to force them open. He found in one drawer a dozen or more bank books, with as many different financial houses, and under many names. This he shoved into his pockets. At last, satisfied that he could gain no more, he retreated to the window. He shut this and was once more on the windowsill. Here he looked down, and a new inspiration came to him. He would have difficulty in getting admission to the apartment entrance, at this time of night. The attendant would remember him and warn Warren upon the latter's return. It was but one more climb, a single story, to the roof. So, up he went, deserting the faithful scaling ladder on the roof, for the time being.

He sought around for several minutes on the snowy, slippery surface before he found the entrance to the iron stairway close by the elevator shaft. Then he went softly down.

Past Warren's apartment, on his way without a noise, his boots off, he continued until he reached the second floor. Here he was baffled again. Why had he not taken some impression of the pass-key of the negro attendant when let in before? Yet now he remembered that the man had never relinquished his hold upon that open sesame. He remembered the "jimmy" - yet this would betray him, by the broken lock!

There was the servant's entrance, however, in the rear of the hallway. To this he slipped, even as the elevator passed up bearing Warren and Shine Taylor, muttering angrily. Shirley found the rear door to the rooms, and there he worked quickly, forcing the lock. He was soon inside, and hid himself in the pantry of the darkened apartment. He had not long to wait.

There was a clicking noise which reverberated through the empty room, as the other two entered by the front portal. He heard them talking in whispers, then the creaking of a window, and all was silent again.

Shirley went to the same small window through which he had descended before. With his boots tied together by their laces, and suspended from his neck, on either side, he went down the rope noiselessly. He found the iron door partially opened, as he reached the end of the corridor. A block of wood held it back from the jamb.

"He is prepared for a quick retreat. So shall I be," thought Shirley, as he noiselessly crept into the chamber, after having drawn away the wooden block. He let the door come gently to its frame, stopping it within an inch of its lock. As he turned slightly forward he caught two curious silhouettes: Warren at his table, with Shine at his side, their outlines clear and black against the brightness of the headlights. On, the other side of the transparent screen stood a man, with one eye blackened, his face badly bruised and wicked in its battered condensation of evil determination with rage and fright, so oddly mixed.

"It ain't my fault, Chief! There are only six of the boys left. I tried me best but this little Chinyman he soaks me one on the lamp, with a gun butt. Me pal was nabbed in the room when I sneaks out on the rope. I finds out afterward that Jimmie's watch must-a been about twenty minutes slow. That's how we misses."

"But you didn't get him, and I'm going to break you for this!"

"But gov'nor, listen - we leaves the machine all right. That'll git 'im anyway. What'll I do?"

"I have the addresses of the other men here in my pocket. You tell them to stick right in their rooms for the next twenty-four hours. If they don't hear anything from me, tell them to go to Frisco by roundabout ways and I'll forward their money, care of Kelso. Now get out."

The man disappeared and there was a double click as the door to the front compartment closed. Warren turned toward Taylor, While Shirley flattened himself against the rear wall, and crouched down slowly, without a betraying sound.

"I don't understand that girl not being there. Some one's closing in on us. I'm going to break that girl's spirit before I'm through. She'll be on the yacht tonight, for everything's ready now. What sort of a machine did you arrange for his room?"

"The old telephone one we worked in Oakland. It is under his bed. I told the men to do that first before they went through his things. Then it would look like plain robbery, and when he goes to take the receiver off the hook it's 'good-night, nursey!' That little popper will blow the roof off that club house!"

Shirley's blood might have run cold at the calm pride of this degenerate fiend, had it not been boiling at the reference to Helene. He crept nearer to them, along the wall. He lay down on the floor, below the level of the first bullet paths. Then he drew his automatic and the bulb light, ready for his surprise.

"I'll call up Kick Brown at the telephone company. He's on duty until twelve. That's an hour yet."

He placed the plug in position but there came no answer over his private wire. Warren cursed: this time in a dialect unknown to Shirley. The man was asserting his most primitive nature now.

"What does that mean? He knows that it's important to-night. I wonder if some one has squealed. You know what I said upstairs, Shine?" Warren's voice was ominous. "I don't like the looks of things. And you're the only one who has ever known the inside working of my system. I've even told you the key to my code - Phil knows it in part, but there is nothing I've kept from you."

Here Shirley's dramatic instinct asserted itself. In a sepulchral voice, he spoke: "One key to the right, in writing. One to the left to read. Hands up, Warren, you're wanted in Paris, and we have the goods on you!"

Placing the bulb light far to his left, he twisted the little catch which kept it glowing permanently. The light fell full on the face of Warren and Taylor as they sprang up back to back!

"Drop that revolver. It's all up now. You go to the chair for these murders."

Warren shot for the body he supposed to be above the little light. As he did so Shirley sent a bullet into the arch criminal's right wrist. The weapon dropped from his hand to the table. Shine Taylor, terror-stricken, staggered against his companion, groping for support. Warren misunderstood it: he thought his assistant was trying to hold him. The swift interpretation gave new fuel to the flame of mistrust which had sprung up in his heart. He knew not how many men were about him - he merely realized that his crafty plans had been set at naught, - there could be only this one explanation. He struck at Taylor, who moaned in pain.

"You cur, you've squealed on me!" With his uninjured left hand he caught the other in his Oriental death grip, with all his consummate skill. Astonished at the sudden move, Shirley rose to his feet. But he hesitated too long.

With a faint gurgle, Shine Taylor, pickpocket, mechanical artist and criminal genius sank to the mouldy ground of the cellar - lifeless!

Shirley snatched up the light, instinctively throwing its rays upon the face of the dead man. It was horrible to see this ghastly ending of the miserable life, so suddenly conceived and grewsomely executed! Here was Warren's opportunity. He caught up his weapon from the table with the left hand, and sent a shot at the intruder, leaping at the same time toward the rear entrance. Monty swung the light about, but the other threw on an electric switch. He stood by the iron portal a fiendish smirk on his distorted features.

"So, my luck is good after all: I've got you where I most want you!" His weapon covered Shirley's. "I shoot as well with my left hand as with my right. But, no, I won't shoot you. I'll put you away without a trace left. That is always the clever way. I told you that the average criminal was too careless about little things. Good-bye, Mr. Montague Shirley, I wish you a pleasant journey!"

His hand, bleeding from the bullet wound, was pushing the iron door, behind him as he faced Shirley. Suddenly a frightful sound broke the stillness: it was the final exhalation of air from the dead man's lungs. It sent a creeping chill through Shirley's blood. Warren's right hand dropped, nervously for an instant, despite his resolution. In that second Shirley had brought his own weapon up to a level with the other's eyes.

The door closed with a clang!

Warren's face lost its sneering smile. He was locked in from the rear!

"Now, let's see you get out the front way," retorted the criminologist. He had one hand behind him. He felt a metal contrivance, With three buttons on it. He thought perhaps it were the controlling switch for the lights. He would take his chances in the dark. He pressed all three quickly.

There was a clang from the front, as some mechanism whirred for an instant. A gong sounded above, and scurrying feet could be heard - then were audible no more. It was the warning alarm for the gangsters: they had fled.

Suddenly to Shirley's straining ears came the tick-ticking of an alarm clock, from the corner of the room to his right. He dare not look at it. Warren's eyes grew black with the Great Fear!

"You fool, you've locked all the entrances, and sent the men away. That clock will ring in exactly five minutes. When it does, this place will go up from a load of lyddite. You've dug your own grave!"

Warren's voice was hoarse, and his bright eyes radiated venomously, as he kept his weapon pointed, like Shirley's, at the face opposite. They were both prisoners in the death cellar, with the advantage in favor of neither!

And the ticking clock, with its maddening, mechanical death chant seemed to Shirley to cry, with each beat, like the reminiscence of some nightmare barbershop: "Next! Next! Next!"

CHAPTER XXIII

CAPTURED AND THEN

Warren's white lips were moving in perfect synchronism, as he counted the seconds and ticks of the clock. Shirley, never so acute, cudgeled his mind for some devise by which he might overcame the other. It was hopeless. At last, just as he knew the inevitable second was almost completed, a faint rustling came from the other side of the iron door. Warren's face brightened with hope. With a nerve-racking rasp, the iron bar on the other side was raised: it was a torturing delay as the two waited!

The door slowly opened. After a harrowing pause a revolver muzzle slid gently through the crack, and a woman's voice murmured softly: "Drop the gun!"

It was Helene Marigold!

Warren's ashen face changed to purple hue, his hand trembled just enough to incite Shirley to a desperate chance. As the criminal drew the trigger with a spasmodic jerk, Shirley was dropping to the floor, whence he pushed himself forward with a froglike leap, as he straightened out the great muscles.

Together they rolled in a frenzied struggle.

"Run back, Helene. The clock will explode!" cried Shirley, desperately. Instead, she sprang into the bright room, espied the diabolical arrangement in the corner, and ran to pick it up.

Eustace Hale Ball

She saw the wire, and her deft fingers reached behind the clock to turn back its hands. Had she torn the wire, as a man would have done, the dreaded explosion would have ended it all.

"We're coming!"

It was the voice of Pat Cleary from the passageway. He rushed through the subterranean passage, followed by several men, with Dick Holloway excitedly in their train. After a titanic struggle, with the man baffled in this maddening moment of ruined triumph, they handcuffed him.

Shirley led Helene into the front compartment before she could observe the horror stamped upon the face of the murdered rogue.

The girl turned her glorious eyes to his, reached forth her hands, and then the eternal feminine conquered as she trembled unsteadily and sank into his arms.

"Break down the doors, Cleary. Out here, to the street. Pull off the hands of that clock - it's a lyddite bomb!" cried Shirley, excitedly.

One of the men used the table with clattering effect. The iron door of the front room gave way, and Shirley carried Helene up the ladder, to the main floor of the old garage. She seemed a sleeping lily - so pale, so fragile, so fragrant in her colorless beauty. He had never seen her so before! For an instant a great terror pierced him: she seemed not to breathe. But as he placed his face close to her mouth, her eyes opened for one divine look, then drooped again. A white hand and arm curled, with childish confidence, about his shoulder. He bore her thus to the big car from the Agency, which stood outside.

"Quick, down to the Hotel California," he called to the chauffeur, "Pat Cleary can handle matters there."

As they sped toward her apartment the roses took their wonted place in her cheeks. She sat up to smile in his face. Then she lowered her glance, with carmine mounting hotly to her brow. Helene said no word - nor did Shirley. She simply leaned toward him, to bury her face upon the broad shoulder, as neither heeded the possible curiosity of the driver on the seat in front.

At least, they understood completely. There was nothing else to say!

* * *

As Shirley left her at the door of the apartment, he turned into the elevator, his mind whirling with the strange imprisonment into which he had let his unwilling heart drift. The clerk stopped him at the lower floor.

"There's a call for you, sir. It's rush, the gentleman said!"

"Great Scott! What now?" he ran to the instrument, and he heard Captain Cronin's excited voice.

"Shirley. The man's escaped again! They just came into the place. He threw some sort of bottle at the front of the patrol wagon which blew it all to pieces. He got away in the mix-up - three policemen were injured!"

"I'll get him, Captain, if it's the last act of my life."

To the surprise of the blase clerk, the well-known club man ran out of the hotel, dropping his hat in his excitement. He shouted to the driver who still waited in the agency machine.

"The sky's the limit, now, son. Race for Twenty-first Street and the East River. Let me off at the end of the dock. Then go back to get some men from the agency, as I'll have a prisoner, then, or they'll get my body!"

The machine raced down the street, regardless of the warnings of policemen. Shirley was confident that his was not the only car on such a mission. He reached the dock of Manby, where was waiting the expert engineer of the hydroplane. He had not planned in vain.

"Have you seen an auto go past here before mine?"

"Yes, sir, I was smoking me pipe, and settin' on the rail of the dock, when one shoots up toward the Twenty-third Street Ferry, with a cop on a motor-cycle chasin' it behind."

"Then, quick, into the boat."

They clambered down the wet ladder, and after an aggravating delay, the whirring engines of the racing craft were started. Shirley took off his coat, and lashed a long rope about his waist. He tied the other end of it securely to a thwart in the boat.

"What's your idee, Cap?" asked the engineer, as he waited the signal.

"There's a man trying to catch that white yacht out in the river. I want to get him, that's all. If I fall out of this boat, keep right on going, for I'm tied up now. Where's the boat hook?"

"Here, sir. Are you ready? Just give me your directions. All right, sir, we're off."

Shirley grunted and the hydroplane sped out onto the river, in a big curve, as he directed. Like a white ghost on the river was the trim yacht, which even now could be seen speeding down the stream, all steam up. There were two toots on the whistle and Shirley feared that his man had boarded her. But the hydroplane, ploughing through the cold waves, whizzed toward the yacht, as he climbed out to the small flat stern. A small boat had swung close to the yacht now. A ladder had been lowered from a spar, while a man standing in the little craft missed it. The yacht was gliding past the boat, when another rope ladder was deftly swung over the stern.

The hydroplane was close up now, and Shirley saw his prey dangling at the end of the ladder, now in the water, struggling with the rungs of the ladder, and now being drawn up.

His engineer, with a skilful hand on the helm, swung in close to the yacht, as keen for the capture as his patron. They whizzed past at almost railroad speed, and Shirley, sprang toward the ladder. His arms closed about the body of Reginald Warren in a grip which he braced by a curious finger-lock he had learned in wrestling practice.

Two revolvers barked over the taffrail of the yacht, as the hydroplane raced onward, dragging Shirley and his prisoner at the end of the rope, through the water. Again the shots rang out, but they were out of range, on the dark waters so quickly, that before the police boat had set out from shore to investigate the firing from the pleasure vessel, the criminologist's struggle with his wounded antagonist was over.

Half drowned, himself, with Warren completely past consciousness, Shirley was pulled into his own boat as the engines were slowed down. They returned rapidly to the dock.

"Help me work him - that was a pretty rough yank. He's been shot in the hand already."

They rolled Warren on a barrel, "pumped" his arms, and by the time the Cronin automobile had returned with the other detectives, Warren was restored to understanding again. Shirley forced some liquor between his teeth, to be greeted with a torrent of strange oaths.

"The jig is up, Warren," said the criminologist. "As a chess-player in the little game, you are a wonder. But, I think I may at last call 'Checkmate.'"

"I'm not dead yet, Shirley," hissed Warren. "I gave you your chance to keep out of this. But you wouldn't take it. I'll settle the score with you before I'm finished. There's one man in the world who knows how to get away from bars. I'm that man."

Then his teeth snapped together with a click. He said nothing more that night, even during the operation for probing Shirley's bullet, and the painful dressing. At the station-house, and his arraignment before the magistrate at Night Court, where he saw some other familiar faces of his fellow gangsters - now rounded up on the same charges - he still maintained that feline silence.

And his eyes never left the face of Montague Shirley, as long as that calm young man was in sight!

Shirley merely presented his charge of murder - for the strangling of Shine Taylor. The names of the aged millionaires were not brought into the matter - there was no need. He had done his work well.

At Cronin's agency, late that night, there came a cablegram from the greatest detective bureau of France.

"The Montfleury case" was the most daring robbery and sale of state war secrets ever perpetrated in Paris. It had been successful, despite the capture, and conviction of the criminal, Laschlas Rozi, a Hungarian adventurer who had killed three men to carry his point. The scoundrel had escaped after murdering his prison guard, and wearing his clothes out of the gaol. A reward of 100,000 francs had been offered for his capture, by the Department of Justice.

"Monty, who gets all the credit for this little deal - that's what's bothering me?" asked Captain Cronin, as they sipped a toast of rare old port, in his rear office.

Shirley lit the ubiquitous cigarette, and tilted back in his chair.

"Captain: why ask foolish questions? This case ought to buy

you five or six of those big farms you've been planning about - and leave you fifty thousand dollars with which to pay the damages for being a gentleman farmer."

"And you, Monty? You know you never have to present a bill with me. What will you do with your pin money?"

"I'm going down on Fifth Avenue tomorrow and invest it in a solitaire ring, for a very small finger."

CHAPTER XXIV

CONCLUSION

Shirley made some investigations in a private reading room of the Public Library: there was much good treasure there, not salable over the counter of a grocery store, mayhap, but unusually valuable in the high grade work which was his specialty. In an old volume enumerating the noble families of Austro-Hungary he found two distinguished lines, "Laschlas" and "Rozi."

From the library he went to a cable office where he sent a message to the chief of police of Budapesth inquiring about the remaining members of the families. The old volume in the library was thirty-four years behind the times: it was the only record obtainable in America.

After a couple of hours, which he devote to some personal matters, he received a response to his inquiry. When translated from the Hungarian it read thus:

"Professor Montague Shirley, College Club, N.Y., U.S.A.

Families extinct except Countess Laschlas, and son Count Rozi Laschlas, reported killed in Albanian revolution.

Csherkini, Minister of Justice."

The criminologist was happy. Here was a weapon which he

had not yet used. Now he turned his steps towards the Tombs, for an interview with the prisoner.

After some parley with the warden, he was admitted for a visit to Reginald Warren. That gentleman's fury was rekindled at the sight of the club man who had been so instrumental in his downfall. But a cunning smile played over the features of the criminal.

"So, you have come to gloat over your work, Shirley? Well, it is a game two can play."

"Yes? I am always interested in sport. I came to see if there was anything I could do for you in your confinement," was the unruffled reply.

"You will be busy with your own affairs," retorted Warren. "I have been busy writing my confession. Here is the manuscript. I will baffle all your efforts to hush up the affairs of the 'Lobster Club.' Furthermore, my confession," (and he exultantly waved a mass of manuscript at his visitor,) "will send young Van Cleft to prison for perjury on the certificate of his father's death. Captain Cronin, that prince of blockheads, will share the same fate. Professor MacDonald, who I know very well signed the death certificates, will be disgraced and driven from professional standing. You will be implicated in this plot to thwart justice. With the German university thoroughness to which you so sarcastically referred, I have written down the facts as carefully as though I were preparing a thesis for a doctor's degree!"

He laughed maliciously, studying the effect of his words. He was disappointed. Shirley's bland manner changed not a whit. Instead the criminologist offered him a cigarette.

"You might as well smoke now - as later!" and there was a wealth of innuendo in the emphasis. "Is that all you are going to do, to square your accounts?"

"By no means! As my trump card, I have implicated Miss Helene Marigold in the various exploits which have been so successful now. She is unknown in New York - I investigated that matter. She will have a fine task in proving an alibi, after the careful preparation I have made. In fact, I accuse her of being the mistress of my dead con'federate - "

Shirley sprang to his feet, and the rage which was shown in his strong features brought a leer to the face of the other.

"Strike me," continued the tormentor. "All I have to do is to call the guard. I have been busy thinking since they locked me up here. There is nothing more to do to me than the electric chair - but, I am not finished yet."

The criminologist controlled himself with difficulty. He realized that an altercation with the prisoner would shatter his whole case, like a house of cards blown down by a vagrant breeze. He sat down again, the mask of calm indifference playing over his features.

"And what then?"

"Is not that sufficient to interest you? It will be another month before my trial, and my literary work has just begun. The newspapers are filled with war news, which have ceased to be a nine days' wonder. I shall provide them with material which will be the story of the age! Another month, and then?"

The prisoner lit the cigarette which he had accepted, and stretched back in the plain wooden chair to enjoy the misery of his victim.

"But, a month - let me see? That would enable me to do some corresponding myself, wouldn't it?" and Shirley took out a memorandum book. "You have degraded a splendid intellect, a gallant spirit and brought disgrace upon yourself, for this miserable ending. You have ruthlessly murdered others, caring naught for the misery and wretchedness of those left behind.

Has it been worth it all, Warren?"

The other's eyes twinkled, as he nodded.

"A wonderful game. And I haven't completed the score, even now."

"You are right, Warren. There is one soul more whom you have not affected. It is too bad that you were not killed in the Albanian revolution, - then you would have been on record as a hero instead of the vilest scoundrel in Christendom."

Had the death-dealing current of the electric chair been turned upon Warren he could not have been more startled, as he sprang up. His pallid face seemed to turn a sickly green, as his dark eyes opened in galvanized amazement.

"Albanian - what do you mean? I never saw Albania!"

"You will never see it again. You will never see Budapesth again, either," was the menacing continuation of the criminologist's methodical speech. "But a very old lady, the Countess Laschlas, will see the accounts of her son's wretched death, in the New York papers which will be sent to her, in care of the American consul!"

It was merely a deductive guess: but the shot struck the center of the bull's-eye. Warren, alias Count Laschlas, staggered back, and his nervous fingers touched the chilling surface of the stone wall. He dropped his eyes, and then strove to regain his nonchalance. It was a pitiable failure.

"Just as you have dealt to the children of others, so will you deal with your own mother, the last of a distinguished line of aristocrats. I swear, by the memory of my own dead parents, that I will avenge the misery you have given to the innocent. The good Book says, the sins of the fathers shall be visited upon the children even unto the third and the fourth generation. But life to-day has taught me that the sins of the children are visited upon the fathers and the mothers - especially, the sweet, loving, trusting mothers! As I value my honor, Reginald Warren, or Count Rozi, I will see to it that your mother shall know every detail of the whole miserable career of her son. That is my answer to your alleged confession. If there is a hereafter, from which you may observe that which follows your death, you will be able to see through eternity the earthly punishment which has been visited upon the one person whom you love and respect."

The criminal's ashen face was buried in his hands.

Great sobs emanated from his white lips, as his shoulders heaved in a paroxysm.

Shirley had struck the Achilles tendon - the hardest wretch in the world had one, as he knew!

"Oh - oh - " he moaned, "the poor little mutter. She has forgiven so much, suffered so much. You can't do it. You won't do it!" He fell to his knees, clawing at the criminologist's garments with his trembling hands, the tears streaming down his face.

"What about those who have seen no compassion from you?" cried Shirley in a terrible voice. "Your vanity, your self-worship! Do they not comfort you now? This is only the suffering of another which you contemplate! Why all these hysterics?"

Warren, groveling on the floor of the reception-room, was a picture of abject, horrid soul-torture. At last, through the subtlety of this unconventional sleuth, along methods which were never dreamed of in the ordinary police category, he had been broken on the wheel which he had himself so cunningly constructed!

"And if that mother dies, cursing your memory with her last breath, cursing the love of the father, of her husband, of the ancestors, all responsible for your being in the world today, what will you think, when you watch from the other side of that great unseen wall?"

"Oh, Shirley! I can't. See - I'll destroy this stuff. I'll keep silent about the others. I mean it. Here: I tear it up now and give you the pieces to burn!"

Warren, maddened by his fears, nervously tore the sheets into bits and pressed the remnants into the criminologist's hands.

"Will you promise to keep my identity a secret?"

"I will not send word to Budapesth. You have a bad record in Paris, and other parts of the world. But, if you play fair on the confidential nature of this case, saving the innocent from disgrace and shame, I will see that the story never reaches your mother. There is no need to ask this on your honor - that does not count."

Warren winced at this final thrust. He turned toward Shirley, eagerly.

"You don't understand me at that, Shirley. I have had a curious career. Somewhere I inherited a strain of criminality - you know how many ancestors a man has in ten generations. I was a member of a poor but prominent family. The government paid for my education in the best universities of Europe, for I was to hold a position under the Emperor, which had been held in my family for generations. But I was ruined by the extravagances and the excesses which I learned from the rich young men whom I met. I studied feverishly, yet was able to waste much time with the gilded fools, by my ability to learn more quickly. The result was that I could not be contented with the small salary of my government office. I had to keep up appearances with my companions. So, I drifted into gambling, into sharp tricks - then became a mercenary soldier, an officer, in the continuous revolutions of the southeastern part of Europe. I sank deeper and at last, in one serious escapade, I managed to have myself reported dead, so as to quiet the heartaches of my mother, who believed I was killed on the battlefield. There is the miserable story - or all I will tell. They caught me in Paris and a girl betrayed part of my name - fortunately they did not hunt me up, so my mother was saved that disgrace. Will you keep the secret now, on our understanding?"

"I give you my word for that, Warren." Shirley rose, putting the torn-up papers into his pockets. "I am sorry for the past - but you have made the present for yourself. Good-bye."

Warren returned to his cell and the detective to the club house.

There he found an additional cable message. It said: "Countess Laschlas has been dead ten months." It was signed like the other.

Shirley tore up the message, and blinked more than seemed necessary.

"Poor little old lady, she knows it all now. I will not have to tell her."

* * *

That afternoon Shirley called again at the Hotel California for Helene.

"I want you to go to a sweet, old-fashioned English tea-room, where I may tell you the rest of the story. There will be no tango music, no cymbals, no tinkling cocktails, nor, champagne. Can you pour real tea?"

"I am an English girl. I have been five days without it."

As they were ensconced at the quaint little table, he realized how wondrously blended in her was that triad of feminine essential spirits: the eternal mother instinct, the sensuous strength of the wife-love and the wistful allurement of maiden tenderness.

"Does my great big boy wish three lumps of sugar, after his hard tasks?"

"He'll die in the flower of immaturity if he has too many sweets in one day."

He drew out his memorandum book, opening it to a closely-written page.

"Before the confections, I must hand in my report to the commanding officer."

"Advance three paces to the front, and hand over the details," and she added another lump of sugar, with a mischievous twinkle in the blue eyes.

"Very well, excellency. We transcribed the addresses of Warren's gangsters from his note-book, and they have all been arrested. The men we captured in the earlier skirmishes are all languishing in the tombs, as accomplices in his crime, as well as for their attempts against my own life. You will be astonished, Helene, at the revelations of his operations as shown by his bank-books, a translation of that diary and some of the letters which I took when I burglarized his rooms. I have sent a code letter to Phil, advising him to confess all, and that man's testimony adds to the corroboration. I went down to the District Attorney with a full statement of the facts, leaving nothing unbared. Like me, he agreed that it were best to let the law take its course, demanding the full penalty, and saving the honor of a dozen families who would have been dragged into the case, had not Warren laid himself liable by the murder of his confederate, Taylor. That young man was an electrical genius - with his brains misguided by his equally misdirected employer. There is no chance of a miscarriage of justice, and Warren had accumulated so much money that many of the victims of his organization can be reimbursed in full."

"You have handled all this with a suspicious skill for a lazy society man, with no experience in such matters."

Shirley understood the subtle sarcasm of the remark, but he proceeded unruffled, to lull her suspicious.

"I only tried to cover the points which meant happiness and peace of mind to others. It was merely a matter of common or garden horse sense, as we call it in America. Warren has been systematically robbing the rich men of New York for three years, under various subterfuges. No wonder he could afford such gorgeous collections of art, keeping aloof from his associates in crime. His treasures, like those in many European museums were bought with blood. It is curious how a complex case like this smooths itself out so simply when the key is obtained. And you, Helene, have been the genius to supply that key: my own work has been merely corroborative!"

He looked at the delicate features of the girl, remembering with a recurring thrill the margin by which they had escaped death in the cellar den of the conspirators.

"Cleary and Dick Holloway told me how cleverly you led the men to the Somerset where you followed my trail through the mole's passage. It was a frightful risk for you to take: Cleary should have had more sense and led the way himself."

Helene's lips pursed themselves into a tempting pout.

"Are you not happier that it was I, at that supreme moment?"

"Indeed I am: success was all the sweeter. There is remaining only one mystery which I must admit is still unsolved in this curious affair. And that is you. Who are you?"

She parried with the same question.

"I know your name, sir, but you profess to be a society butterfly, flitting from pleasure to dissipation, and back again.

Tell me the truth, now, if ever."

"Why - gracious, Helene - of all the foolish questions!" He was adorably boyish in his confusion. She laughed gleefully, like a happy schoolgirl.

"Then, Monty Shirley, my score is better than yours, for I have every mystery cleared. But while I know all about you, what frightful chances you are taking with me!"

Shirley reddened, as he burned his finger with the match which had been raised to the end of his cigarette. He accused her of teasing, and she glanced happily at the iridiscent solitaire upon the third finger of her left hand.

"Dear boy, I realize that I understand about you what you cannot fathom with me. You are not a moth, but your self-sacrifice, and bravery in this case are professional: you worked on this case as you have on a hundred others: you are a very original and successful expert in criminology. And I am not more than half bad at observation and deduction, myself; now, am I, dear?"

Shirley gracefully admitted defeat, with a question: "Who are you, Helene? And who is dear old Jack?"

The roses blossomed in her cheeks as she answered: "Jack is a very sweet boy, ten years older than you in gray hair and the calendar, and infinitely younger in worldly wisdom and intellect. He is an English army officer, who was foolish enough to imagine he loved me, foolish enough to propose every three days for the last three years and foolish enough to bore me until in self-defense I escaped from his clutches. As for myself, at least I am not the young woman who can stand staying in that gaudy theatrical hotel for another day longer. I have done so many bold, unmaidenly things that you may believe it easy for me. It is not.

"I am truly a horrid, old-time, hoopskirt-minded prude. My

first act of domestic tyranny is to make you find a sedate, prim place for my work and play, where I may know my own blushes when I see them in the mirror, and will have less occasion to deserve them!"

"Your work? What is that?"

"It is very hard work - with a typewriter, but not in code. I will not divulge my name until we tell it to the marriage license clerk. But Dick Holloway knows me, and I came to this country, partly to see him. I have written a few plays, which simple as they were, seemed to interest European audiences and critics. Some of my novels have strangely enough brought in royalties, despite the publishers! But, I became satiated with life in England and on the Continent. I came here because I felt that I needed life in a younger and newer country. I needed an emotional and physical awakening."

"You have not wasted any time in drowsiness since you reached America."

"No - and all because I went to Holloway's office that fateful morning, before I saw any one else in New York, to ask about a play which he is to produce this spring. I confess that it was my first experience as an actress. Will you forgive my deception?"

Shirley nodded, as he studied the animated face with a new interest. He admitted to himself that Holloway's prediction had come true - he had met his match.

"And so, my dear Helene (for such I shall always call you, whether your really, truly name be Mehitabel, Samantha or Sophronisa) you came here, went through all these horrors without a complaint, crushing the independence of my confirmed bachelorhood for the sake of what we newspaper men call copy?"

Helene nodded demurely.

"Yes, but it was such wonderful 'copy,' Monty boy."

The criminologist scowled over his cigarette, yet he could not feel as unhappy as he felt this defeat should make him.

"When will the 'copy' be ready for publication, my dear girl. It would be most interesting, I fancy."

Helene caught his hand, drawing it toward her throbbing heart. Her wet lips were almost touching his ear, as she confided, whisperingly, with the blue eyes averted: "Only published in editions de luxe: some bindings will be with blue ribbons, some with pink. All of them with flexible backs and gloriously illumined by the Master's brush. The authors' autographs will be on every copy to prove the collaboration, and every volume will be a poem in itself .... But there, Montague dear, I am a novelist - not a fortune-teller!"

"How can I forecast the exact dates of publication?"

Choose from Thousands of 1stWorldLibrary Classics By

Ada Leverson
Adolphus William Ward
Aesop
Agatha Christie
Alexander Aaronsohn
Alexander Kielland
Alexandre Dumas
Alfred Gatty
Alfred Ollivant
Alice Duer Miller
Alice Turner Curtis
Alice Dunbar
Ambrose Bierce
Amelia E. Barr
Andrew Lang
Andrew McFarland Davis
Andy Adams
Anna Sewell
Annie Besant
Annie Hamilton Donnell
Annie Payson Call
Annonaymous
Anton Chekhov
Arnold Bennett
Arthur Conan Doyle
Arthur M. Winfield
Arthur Ransome
Atticus
B.H. Baden-Powell
B. M. Bower
Baroness Emmuska Orczy
Baroness Orczy
Basil King
Bayard Taylor
Ben Macomber
Bertha Muzzy Bower
Bjornstjerne Bjornson
Booth Tarkington
Boyd Cable
Bram Stoker
C. Collodi
C. E. Orr
C. M. Ingleby
Carolyn Wells
Catherine Parr Traill
Charles A. Eastman
Charles Dickens
Charles Dudley Warner
Charles Farrar Browne

Charles Ives
Charles Kingsley
Charles Klein
Charles Lathrop Pack
Charles Whibley
Charles Willing Beale
Charlotte M. Braeme
Charlotte M. Yonge
Charlotte Perkins Stetson
Clair W. Hayes
Clarence Day Jr.
Clarence E. Mulford
Clemence Housman
Confucius
Cornelis DeWitt Wilcox
Cyril Burleigh
D. H. Lawrence
Daniel Defoe
David Garnett
Don Carlos Janes
Donald Keyhoe
Dorothy Kilner
Dougan Clark
Douglas Fairbanks
E. Nesbit
E.P.Roe
E. Phillips Oppenheim
Edgar Rice Burroughs
Edith Van Dyne
Edith Wharton
Edward J. O'Biren
Edward S. Ellis
Edwin L. Arnold
Eleanor Atkins
Eliot Gregory
Elizabeth Gaskell
Elizabeth McCracken
Elizabeth Von Arnim
Ellem Key
Emerson Hough
Emily Dickinson
Enid Bagnold
Enilor Macartney Lane
Erasmus W. Jones
Ernie Howard Pie
Ethel Turner
Ethel Watts Mumford
Eugenie Foa
Eugene Wood

Evelyn Everett-green
Everard Cotes
F. H. Cheley
F. J. Cross
Federick Austin Ogg
Ferdinand Ossendowski
Francis Bacon
Francis Darwin
Frances Hodgson Burnett
Frances Parkinson Keyes
Frank Gee Patchin
Frank Harris
Frank Jewett Mather
Frank L. Packard
Frank V. Webster
Frederic Stewart Isham
Frederick Trevor Hill
Frederick Winslow Taylor
Friedrich Kerst
Friedrich Nietzsche
Fyodor Dostoyevsky
G.A. Henty
G.K. Chesterton
Gabrielle E. Jackson
Garrett P. Serviss
Gaston Leroux
George Ade
Geroge Bernard Shaw
George Durston
George Ebers
George Eliot
George MacDonald
George Meredith
George Orwell
George Tucker
George W. Cable
George Wharton James
Gertrude Atherton
Grace E. King
Grace Gallatin
Grant Allen
Guillermo A. Sherwell
Gulielma Zollinger
Gustav Flaubert
H. A. Cody
H. B. Irving
H.C. Bailey
H. G. Wells
H. H. Munro

H. Irving Hancock	James DeMille	Louisa May Alcott
H. Rider Haggard	James Joyce	Lucy Fitch Perkins
H. W. C. Davis	James Lane Allen	Lucy Maud Montgomery
Hamilton Wright Mabie	James Lane Allen	Lydia Miller Middleton
Hans Christian Andersen	James Oliver Curwood	Lyndon Orr
Harold Avery	James Oppenheim	M. Corvus
Harold McGrath	James Otis	M. H. Adams
Harriet Beecher Stowe	James R. Driscoll	Margaret E. Sangster
Harry Houidini	Jane Austen	Margaret Vandercook
Helent Hunt Jackson	Jens Peter Jacobsen	Margret Penrose
Helen Nicolay	Jerome K. Jerome	Maria Edgeworth
Hendrik Conscience	John Burroughs	Maria Thompson Daviess
Hendy David Thoreau	John Cournos	Mariano Azuela
Henri Barbusse	John F. Kennedy	Marion Polk Angellotti
Henrik Ibsen	John Gay	Mark Overton
Henry Adams	John Glasworthy	Mark Twain
Henry Ford	John Habberton	Mary Austin
Henry Frost	John Joy Bell	Mary Catherine Crowley
Henry James	John Kendrick Bangs	Mary Cole
Henry Jones Ford	John Milton	Mary Hastings Bradley
Henry Seton Merriman	John Philip Sousa	Mary Roberts Rinehart
Henry W Longfellow	Jonas Lauritz Idemil Lie	Mary Rowlandson
Herbert A. Giles	Jonathan Swift	M. Wollstonecraft Shelley
Herbert N. Casson	Joseph A. Altsheler	Maud Lindsay
Herman Hesse	Joseph Carey	Max Beerbohm
Homer	Joseph Conrad	Myra Kelly
Honore De Balzac	Joseph E. Badger Jr	Nathaniel Hawthrone
Horace Walpole	Joseph Hergesheimer	Nicolo Machiavelli
Horatio Alger Jr.	Joseph Jacobs	O. F. Walton
Howard Pyle	Julian Hawthrone	Oscar Wilde
Howard R. Garis	Julies Vernes	Owen Johnson
Hugh Lofting	Justin Huntly McCarthy	P.G. Wodehouse
Hugh Walpole	Kakuzo Okakura	Paul and Mabel Thorne
Humphry Ward	Kenneth Grahame	Paul G. Tomlinson
Ian Maclaren	Kenneth McGaffey	Paul Severing
Inez Haynes Gillmore	Kate Langley Bosher	Percy Brebner
Irving Bacheller	Kate Langley Bosher	Peter B. Kyne
Israel Abrahams	Katherine Cecil Thurston	Plato
Ivan Turgenev	Katherine Stokes	R. Derby Holmes
J.G.Austin	L. A. Abbot	R. L. Stevenson
J. Henri Fabre	L. T. Meade	R. S. Ball
J. M. Barrie	L. Frank Baum	Rabindranath Tagore
J. Macdonald Oxley	Latta Griswold	Rahul Alvares
J. S. Fletcher	Laura Lee Hope	Ralph Henry Barbour
J. S. Knowles	Laurence Housman	Ralph Waldo Emmerson
J. Storer Clouston	Leo Tolstoy	Rene Descartes
Jack London	Leonid Andreyev	Rex Beach
Jacob Abbott	Lewis Carroll	Rex E. Beach
James Allen	Lilian Bell	Richard Harding Davis
James Andrews	Lloyd Osbourne	Richard Jefferies
James Baldwin	Louis Tracy	Richard Le Gallienne

Robert Barr
Robert Frost
Robert Gordon Anderson
Robert L. Drake
Robert Lansing
Robert Lynd
Robert Michael Ballantyne
Robert W. Chambers
Rosa Nouchette Carey
Rudyard Kipling
Samuel B. Allison
Samuel Hopkins Adams
Sarah Bernhardt
Selma Lagerlof
Sherwood Anderson
Sigmund Freud
Standish O'Grady
Stanley Weyman
Stella Benson
Stephen Crane
Stewart Edward White
Stijn Streuvels
Swami Abhedananda

Swami Parmananda
T. S. Ackland
T. S. Arthur
The Princess Der Ling
Thomas A. Janvier
Thomas A Kempis
Thomas Anderton
Thomas Bailey Aldrich
Thomas Bulfinch
Thomas De Quincey
Thomas H. Huxley
Thomas Hardy
Thomas More
Thornton W. Burgess
U. S. Grant
Valentine Williams
Various Authors
Victor Appleton
Virginia Woolf
Walter Camp
Walter Scott
Washington Irving
Wilbur Lawton

Wilkie Collins
Willa Cather
Willard F. Baker
William Dean Howells
William le Queux
W. Makepeace Thackeray
William W. Walter
Winston Churchill
Yei Theodora Ozaki
Yogi Ramacharaka
Young E. Allison
Zane Grey

www.ingramcontent.com/pod-product-compliance
Lightning Source LLC
Chambersburg PA
CBHW030314180626
46810CB00003B/1066